Reese

Reese

A BAY AREA DUET SERIES NOVELLA

PERSEPHONE AUTUMN

BETWEEN WORDS PUBLISHING LLC

Reese

ISBN: 978-1-951477-54-7 (Ebook)

ISBN: 978-1-951477-55-4 (Paperback)

ISBN: 978-1-951477-56-1 (Hardcover)

Editor: Ellie McLove | My Brother's Editor

Proofreader: Rosa Sharon | My Brother's Editor

Cover Design: Persephone Autumn | Between Words Publishing LLC

To those who were scared to love, but took the leap.

Love is love is love.
And you are loved.

Lake Lavender Series

Depths Awakened

One Night Forsaken

Every Thought Taken

Devotion Series

Distorted Devotion

Undying Devotion

Beloved Devotion

Darkest Devotion

Sweetest Devotion

Bay Area Duet Series

Click Duet

Through the Lens

Time Exposure

Inked Duet

Fine Line

Love Buzz

Insomniac Duet

Restless Night

A Love So Bright

Artist Duet

Blank Canvas

Abstract Passion

Novellas

Reese

Penny

Stone Bay Series

Broken Sky — Prequel

Standalone Romance Novels

Sweet Tooth

Transcendental

Poetry Collections

Ink Veins

Broken Metronome

Slipping From Existence

PUBLISHED UNDER P. AUTUMN

Standalone Non-Romance Novels

By Dawn

ONE

REESE

Never thought I'd see this day, yet here it is, slapping me in the face. Hard. Reminding me that I played the field far too long and took people for granted. Nagging me that it is time to grow up and settle down.

Too bad the man I want to settle with isn't here.

Once again, Trent is gone. Away on business. Flying across the US to oversee the next construction site in his business empire. A mirror image of the one in Tampa, just thousands of miles away.

I should be happy for him. Should congratulate him on the feats he has accomplished. Should be his biggest cheerleader as he nears the top of the wealthiest-people list in the Bay Area. He worked hard to get where he is and I should applaud his diligence.

Instead, I sit in my dark living room, surrounded by filth, pouting. Berating myself and my decisions.

Trent left three days ago for California. Told me he

1

would be gone five days. As with every previous trip, he basically broke things off. Gave me permission to hook up with other people, guilt-free.

And I hate it. Hate his easy dismissal of me, of us. Hate that every time he does this, it feels like a knife to the chest. An effortless rejection that slashes and scars and fucking hurts for days. Makes me feel disposable and worthless.

"We don't need to do this." I wave my hands between us. *"Break up every time you go out of town."*

He rubs the back of his neck, averts his gaze, and sighs. "Reese, I don't want you to feel obligated or tied to me when I'm not here." His eyes close as he takes a deep breath. "And I'm gone more often than not." Dark-green irises meet mine, a silent plea in them begging me to understand. To accept and drop the argument. "It isn't fair to you. Don't limit yourself because I can't be here."

Irritation heats my skin as I consider his words. Play them over and over and let them sink in. Is it me who is limited or him? Maybe he does this every time because he doesn't want to feel guilty for any acts he commits when he goes out of town.

"You sure it's me you're worried about?" I ask before I lose the nerve.

His brows pinch together, his eyes narrowing. "Not sure I follow."

"If I complain about us breaking up every trip you take, I don't think it's me who feels limited." Without outright saying it, I insinuate he is the one who doesn't want limitations. He doesn't want to be obligated or tied down. Because maybe his trips have more side adventures than I realize.

"Say what you mean, Reese," he bites out. "We're grown men.

No sense in skirting around how we feel." His face reddens as he works his jaw.

Braving a step forward, I swallow past the lump in my throat. Ignore the pang in my gut and building sweat on my brow. Take a deep breath and straighten my spine as I open my mouth to speak my truth.

"Are you sleeping with other people? While you're gone, I mean."

God, now that it is out in the open, I feel foolish. Immature and needy. Like a damn jealous nag.

Minutes pass as Trent simply stares. His face is void of expression. No hurt or shame or anger. No disbelief or confusion or humor. He's just… blank.

And damn if it doesn't throw my head into more of a tailspin.

On the verge of walking away, I study him for one last deep breath. Scrutinize his impassive expression. Stab. With a shake of my head, I step back, pivot, and start my retreat. I don't need this bullshit. I don't deserve this bullshit.

On the second step, a hand wraps around my bicep.

"Wait," Trent whispers. "Please."

I halt my retreat but don't spin to face him. Not yet.

"Are you?" I ask again.

His hand falls away, but the heat of him remains. A constant reminder Trent is more than anyone that came before him. Trent is who I want. Who I need. If only my affections were reciprocated. If only luck were on my side.

"No, Reese," he answers, sadness softening his voice. "I don't have sex with or date others while I'm gone."

I spin around at a dizzying speed. Drag a hand through my hair. Open my mouth to speak, then snap it shut as my mind races. Sucking in a deep breath, I close my eyes, count to three, and pray for clarity. As my eyes open, Trent runs a hand over his mouth and jaw.

"Then why?" The two-word question laced with incredulity. "Why all the dramatics when you leave? I… help me understand."

He steps into me, invades every ounce of my personal space, and frames my face with his hands. I gasp from the simple yet intimate touch. Because all I want to do is kiss him. Kiss him and make all this nonsense end. Kiss him and tell him with my lips I want no one except him.

But I don't move.

"How long have we been together now?" His question is rhetorical, so I don't answer. "Close to a year. Unless I discount my time away." He inches closer, his breath warm on my lips. "I hate leaving you. Hate that I'm gone a week or two at a time, and you're just here, waiting for me to return." On a deep inhale, he shakes his head. "It isn't fair to you. To sit and wait. To wish I was here. So, I give you a pass. Give you the freedom to do as you please, without guilt."

"But you're wrong," I whisper with my eyes on his lips. "You say the words, but there is no pass. Not really. Because the moment you return, we're right back where we left off."

He inches back and pinches the bridge of his nose. "This will get old, Reese."

"For who?" I rear back and meet his gaze as his hands clap his sides. "Because it sounds like you're fishing for excuses now."

Trent steps back, and I shiver at the chilled look on his face. "I don't need to make excuses, Reese," he bites out with more volume. He checks his watch and huffs out a breath. "And I don't have time to argue." He turns away and walks toward the bedroom.

"So that's it?" I ask, following in his wake. "You don't have time, so the conversation is done?"

He pops up the handle on his carry-on suitcase and wheels it out of the room. "No, of course not. But I have a flight to catch. I can't spend the next several hours debating this."

"When?"

He pockets his wallet, keys, and phone. "When, what?"

"When will we finish this conversation? Because it needs to happen."

He checks his watch again, and I want to scream. It has been maybe a minute since he last looked.

"When I'm back," he states, unlocking and opening the front door.

"Which is . . ."

"Five days."

Five days. I can hold off for five days. It isn't the longest he's been away. "Fine. Have a safe trip. See you when you're back."

Without another word, Trent leaves. The immediate silence is deafening. The sharp pain in my chest is excruciating. And with each new breath, I wilt from his absence. With every heartbeat, I shrink in on myself.

It's only five days. He'll be back in no time and we'll talk.

Five days.

Three days have come and gone without a word from Trent. On most of his trips, I get texts or picture updates. Small check-ins that let me know he thinks of me, that he cares.

This time around, nothing. Complete radio silence. And I hate it with every cell in my body. Hate the rift that suddenly exists between us. Hate that our relationship was left on a sour note. More than anything, I hate the feeling beneath my diaphragm. The one that begs me to reach out and initiate contact, but I fear it will do more damage than good.

His silence has taken its toll. Made me question if staying with him is really what I want or deserve. With each passing second, the gray cloud following me in his absence grows darker. Thicker. Angrier. Miserable.

I need to do something to fix this, fix us. Help us find balance in our off-kilter lives. Help us find a middle ground. A place where we can be together and not feel at odds.

Trent leads a busy life, but his workload is a lame excuse for us to not move forward. Countless couples with hectic schedules have meaningful, happy relationships. If he didn't care, he would let me go. And he hasn't. Not completely.

Deep in my bones, I know we will make this work. He just needs proof. Needs to be shown that if we both want this, us, we will overcome every obstacle thrown our way. Together.

Whatever it takes.

Because, dammit, I don't want a day without him.

TWO

TRENT

Hands gripping the armrests, I jolt forward as the plane touches down in Tampa. No matter how many times I've flown, I still hate landings.

The pilot steers the plane toward the gate then slows to a stop. Clinks echo in the cabin as passengers unbuckle their seat belts, rise and fumble for their carry-ons. Everyone except me. Although I want off the plane, I am in no rush. Not with what awaits once I deplane.

"I fucked up," I mumble.

For the first time, I despise my job. Despise the guilt over being busy nonstop, something I once enjoyed. Most of all, I despise the ache in my chest every time I walk away from Reese. The hurt I cause him.

Before him, there was never a dull ache beneath my breastbone. Never a doubt about what I wanted from life. Never an impulse to give up everything to spend time with someone.

Now, my need for him is inescapable. A living,

breathing life force. Something I won't exist without. I love and hate the hold he has on my heart. This unrelenting fist wrapped around the small organ in my chest. Reese gives me a new sense of purpose. New reasons to smile. But being with him also makes me irrational and unsteady and skeptical.

How the hell can our relationship move past sex and the occasional dinner together? How can we survive as a couple when I am often absent?

As the plane empties, I rise from my seat and stretch my limbs. Fishing my carry-on from the overhead compartment, I extend the handle and inch toward the exit. With each step forward, my stomach twists in a new knot. With each step forward, my breaths turn more jagged.

Only one person will ease this ache. Only one person will soothe the uncertainty. And damn, do I regret the last words we exchanged. Words that punched me in the gut. Words bearing resemblance to the end.

Please, whoever is listening, I beg you, don't let this be the end.

I should have called or texted him.

Mentally, I berate myself as I park next to Reese's car. We haven't spoken in five days, yet I assume it is perfectly acceptable to show up on his doorstep unannounced. Assume he wants to see me after how we left things.

Idiot.

What if he isn't alone? What if he actually took my words to heart and spent time with someone else? In the heat of the moment, I said something I didn't mean. Told him he had a free pass when I left. All but handed him a permission slip to be promiscuous.

What if, in a moment of anger or to spite me, he followed through? What if he *slept* with someone else?

Bile rises in my throat at the thought, but I shove it down. "No," I whisper to myself. "He wouldn't." Not after he fought so hard to keep what we have.

Leaving the suitcase in the car, I put one foot in front of the other and follow the path to Reese's front door. Sweat slicks my brow and temples as my heart pound, pound, pounds a vicious rhythm in my chest. Each step feels a mile long until I reach the door. My pulse kicks into fifth gear, the whooshing behind my ears all I hear.

Fuck. I am going to puke.

Bracing a hand on the wall, I close my eyes and take a deep breath. Then another. When the ground feels more stable beneath my feet, I open my eyes.

Everything will be fine. Once we talk, it will all be okay.

Knuckles meet metal as I knock on the door. My other hand drums my thigh as I wait for Reese to open the door. *Tap, tap, tap. Tap, tap, tap.* The concept of time vanishes as I wait for him to answer. Wait to see him, speak with him, touch him. When he doesn't answer, I knock again, this time with more gusto.

On the other side of the door, I hear a groan. *Or was that a moan?*

My heart drops. A fresh dose of acid trickles up and burns my throat.

Before I can bolt, the door swings open and I stop breathing.

Devilishly sexy, Reese stands shirtless in the doorway with his dark, curly locks rumpled. His skin slightly red and damp. Breath ragged and pulse pounding hard enough to see the vein throb in his neck.

Fuck, fuck, fuck. Too late. I am too damn late. We fought and I dismissed him. And now, he is done with me, with us. He took my words to heart and moved on.

Fuck.

I open my mouth to speak, but can't find my voice. Can't breathe. Can't think. Bending at the waist, I grip my knees and try to suck in a breath. Try to ease the sudden panic taking hold. My lungs burn as the world spins and I close my eyes.

"Shit." The word echoes in my ears as warm arms snake around my middle. "Breathe, T. Nice and slow. I got you."

I do as Reese says. One breath at a time, cool air fills my lungs. One breath at a time, my wobbly world stabilizes. With a stronger foothold, I inch back to my full height and open my eyes. Take in the room. Register during my momentary haze, Reese guiding us into his apartment.

Is he alone? God, please let him be alone.

"I... uh..." Scanning the apartment, I spot several take-out containers and beer bottles on the coffee table.

The room dimly lit from the barely cracked blinds. "Sorry," I mutter.

Reese turns away from me and ambles into the kitchen without a word. I press my thumb and finger to my temples before finger-combing my hair as I take in the space again.

The apartment is a disaster. Reese isn't the tidiest human on the planet, but I have never seen his space in such disarray. Chinese food cartons, pizza boxes, ice cream containers. *Hope those are empty.* Beer bottles and energy drink cans. Mugs and paper plates and plastic utensils. Clothes on the table and couch and trailing down the hall. Envelopes and grocery store adverts on the floor.

I wrinkle my nose. *What the hell is that smell?* Like a mix of curdled milk and body odor and something else.

Blech.

"Sorry for what?" Reese asks as he exits the kitchen and hands me a bottle of water.

"Thanks." I take a long pull from the bottle before twisting the cap back in place. "Where do I begin?" I laugh without humor, and Reese stares at me with the blankest expression. I take in his sweat-slicked skin and can't hold back what I say next. "Are you alone?"

His eyes drop to his chest and he scowls. "Not that you deserve an answer, but yes. Was just trying to get out of my head. Thought maybe time on the treadmill would help."

Stupid, stupid, stupid.

Just because I created this fracture in our relationship doesn't mean Reese deepened the crack. If anything, he wanted to stitch us back together. Make us whole. And I refused him the time to do so.

"I fucked up," I blurt out. "And I shouldn't have left the way I did. It was wrong. *I* was wrong."

Reese nods but doesn't say a word. Not in agreement or to refute. And I deserve every bit of his silence. Every ounce of his torment.

"Can we please talk?" I ask, my tone pleading.

Again, he nods, then walks toward the living room. He shoves shirts and socks aside on the couch but makes no move to clear the trash on the table. Parking on the far end of the couch, he angles himself in my direction before crossing his arms over his chest. I take a seat, not quite at the other end of the couch, but also not the middle.

He needs space.

"I fucked up," I repeat. Feels as if I will reiterate this for weeks to come. "Relationships aren't my strong suit, obviously. Between my office hours and the constant travel, I've never had time for anyone. Never had someone I needed to make time for." I shake my head, eyes downcast as my fingers peel away the water bottle label. "But I want to make time for you." My brows pinch then relax as I look up and hold his stare. His tawny irises unwavering as they watch every word form on my lips. "It's just…" I close my eyes and search for what to say, but nothing seems sufficient.

"It's just what?"

My eyes open to meet his as I hear the slight change in his tone. Concern, maybe?

"How?" I lean forward, set the bottle on the floor,

drop my elbows to my knees and put my face in my hands. My fingers lightly bruise the skin of my forehead before diving into my hair and tugging the strands. "How do I balance everything?" I straighten and give one last tug of my hair before holding my hands out. "How is it fair if I can't be what you need? If I can't be *here* when you need?"

The room falls silent once more as my words float through the air. As they sink in and take root.

This is why I never give myself over to someone fully. It isn't that I don't *want* to commit to someone. It's my lack of free time that keeps me from taking the next step.

Not being present... no one wants a nonexistent partner. Absence steals the possibility of healthy, long-term connections. So why put in the effort? Why hurt ourselves?

"Do I get a say?" he asks, voice gruff and pained. "Do I get a choice?" His voice a touch louder now as he shifts in his seat. "Yeah, when all this started"—he gestures between us—"I didn't expect it to be more than one night. Maybe two." Looking away from me, he works his jaw. "But here we are."

His eyes meet mine and I *feel* his ache. See his hurt in his glassy stare. And fuck... it burns like a hot branding iron to the heart.

"Here we are," I parrot on a whisper. I swallow past the dryness in my throat. Swallow past the nerves fizzling beneath the surface. "Of course, you get a say." I hang my head and stare at the stitch lines of the couch fabric. "But I don't want you to resent me," I admit, voice almost inaudible. "Ever."

The couch cushion wobbles slightly as Reese inches closer. Comfort I have no right to feel blankets me as he lays a hand on my knee. His thumb draws small circles and I bask in that simple touch. Delight in the fire that stirs just beneath the surface. Revel in the man that makes me feel more alive now than any day before he entered my life.

And god... I don't deserve him. Don't deserve his affection or forgiveness. But here he is, gifting me both.

Because Reese Triggs is a good man. A man worthy of much more than I give him. Oh, how I want to deserve him. How I want to be worthy of his heart.

"Our relationship may not fit some preconceived mold, but I don't care."

I lift my gaze to his. See the sincerity of his words in the set of his features. Feel the conviction of his words vibrating off him. And I do my best to soak it all in. Let his truth settle in my bones. Let it fill my lungs and pump my heart. I allow myself to believe him.

Because I want nothing more.

To be with Reese.

To *love* him.

For him to love me in return.

"Okay." I roll my lips between my teeth. "But how will this work?" My eyes drop to his lips and damn, I want to kiss him. Want to wrap him in my arms and ravage him breathless. But before I lose complete focus, I snap my eyes back to his. Concentrate on our conversation and think of how to make this work with him. "I work insane hours. Fly across the country for days at a time." With a soft shake of my head, I sigh. "How is that acceptable? You'd only have me for small slivers of time."

Every time I leave Reese, a new splinter etches my heart. It isn't only him suffering, but I don't dare act selfish in this moment. Don't compare my misery to his. They aren't the same.

When I started Centro Collective, I never imagined it growing to what it is today. A large-scale operation. Booming. Thriving. Fulfilling an undiscovered need.

Before I spoke full sentences, Dad had been shaping me to take over Callahan Financial and Associates. His father passed the business to him and he wanted to do the same. Pass a legacy torch. For years, I'd been convinced no other career path was suitable. No other career would bring me joy. Callahan Financial was endgame.

Until I saw a need.

Fresh out of college, I'd been working for my father's investment firm for six months. I'd had an appointment with a client that requested we meet outside the office. It was a first, but I agreed without hesitation. The man was a major player. Someone I needed to keep on my roster. Someone Callahan Financial wanted to keep happy.

So I drove more than an hour to meet him. We sat at a secluded table in the back of a coffee shop. And as we'd gone over investments, I'd surveyed the room. Taken in how many other people were talking business with a cup of coffee or tea and a bite to eat. Questioned why there wasn't a better place for meetings.

That day, my vision of Centro Collective was born. A place where people can meet with privacy. A place where professionals without storefronts can rent space to work from when necessary.

From the start, it has blown up. Taken on a life of its own. Morphed into more than I imagined possible.

Some of my travel is to curate items for the buildings. Other trips are to oversee new Centro Collective structures coming to life. What started as an idea has slowly turned into an empire. Being the head of it all is a thrill. Earning the title "Top-Tier Entrepreneur of the Bay Area" was a bonus.

But what have I sacrificed for said power?

"I'll take what I can get," Reese says, snapping me back into focus.

"Why?"

I don't mean to question him, but I need to know. Why is he so willing to take small percentages when someone else can give him one hundred percent? The notion seems ludicrous.

He lifts his hands and cups my jaw in both. Strokes his thumbs over my cheeks. Steals my breath as his penetrating gaze locks with mine. Then, ever so slowly, he leans forward to kiss my lips.

"Because I'm in love with you."

THREE

REESE

Did I say I'm in love with him? Out loud?

Shit.

Before I wrap my head around my confession, he frames my face, hauls me forward and crushes my lips with his. My stiff muscles loosen as his lips dance over mine. My pulse thunders beneath my sternum for a new reason. Every dark and panicked thought to cross my mind in his absence is replaced with warmth and light and love. Every worry I harbored about my feelings not being reciprocated evaporates.

He hasn't said the words back, but this kiss… Trent Callahan loves me too.

I groan when he breaks the kiss. A breathy chuckle leaves his lips as he drops his forehead to mine, our labored breaths floating between us.

Soft thumbs stroke the stubble on my cheeks. Slow and rhythmic. Hypnotic and gentle. On instinct, I melt into his touch. His affection. Him.

God, I missed him. Terribly.

"Never want to fight again," I mutter, reaching for his shirt and fisting the fabric in my hands.

"Me either." A chaste kiss presses my lips. "And I…"

I stop breathing as I wait for him to finish his thought. As I wait for him to tell me he feels the same. That he is in love with me too.

But with his hesitation, the room turns deathly silent. A chill sweeps over my skin as the weight of his silence suffocates me. Pulls me under and refuses to let go.

Inching back, I break the physical connection. Put several inches between us and take a deep breath.

I am a goddamn fool. He doesn't love me. Not in the way I want him to. How can he?

Rising from the couch, I step around the coffee table and aim my feet toward the hall.

Less than twenty steps and I will be in my room. Less than twenty steps and I will escape this awkward, one-sided love confession.

But I don't make it far. On my third step, Trent bolts from the couch and darts around the other side of the table, blocking my path.

"Please don't walk away." His eyes widen with panic. His chest rising and falling faster with each breath.

I want to cave to his wishes. Want to stand here with him, be here with him, love him, but fuck… it hurts. It hurts to expose yourself to someone, spill your heart at their feet, and not get an inkling in return. Yes, he kissed me as if he were confessing his love. But he hasn't *said* anything.

Should I expect him to say he loves me too? Absolutely not, and I didn't assume he would. I shouldn't need to hear the words, but I want them. Something, *anything*, to let me know he wants more than the occasional hookup and slumber party with cuddles would be a comfort.

"I don't know what else to do."

"Give me a minute." He holds up a finger. "Please. I have more to say and, for the first time in my life, I can't seem to articulate a damn word." He laughs without humor, a slight shake of his head. "Please, Reese." His glassy eyes plead more than his words. "All I ask is you give me a moment. Let me try to get what I'm feeling out."

I step into him, my gaze locked on his evergreen irises. "Yeah. Okay."

We move back to the couch and I send a silent petition to the universe. *Please, don't let this man crush my heart.*

After hours of conversation and confessions, a new tranquility blankets my heart.

The first thirty minutes, Trent expressed his concerns over our relationship moving forward. Difficult as it was to remain tight lipped and not counter his justification to stay casual, I kept my thoughts to myself and gave him the floor.

With his chaotic schedule, Trent harbors a world of guilt for not being able to devote more time to me or our relationship. When he said his piece, I jumped in headfirst and squashed his reasons immediately. I explained how I knew what I was getting into as our relationship evolved. He argued and I opposed. When I told him his passion and drive and tenacity were reasons why I loved him, he cut off the debate.

And then words I didn't expect from him so soon came tumbling out.

"I love you, Reese. And it scares me to no end."

The next hour was spent exploring why he feared loving me. More than anything, his apprehension stems from his inability to be present enough. His inability to provide me with what I need emotionally.

"I don't want you to wake up one day and resent me for not being what you hoped for or needed."

Our conversation ended long ago, but we haven't made a move to leave the couch. His head on my shoulder, our arms hooked at the elbow, his sweet, woodsy scent is a balm for my soul. I close my eyes and breathe him in as the room grows darker from the setting sun.

For the first time since he walked out the door five days ago, the world feels more stable. As if my knees won't buckle. As if I won't crumble each time I wake up alone.

"I'm in this for the long haul," I whisper into the fading light of day.

He nods subtly, giving me more of his weight. "Just bear with me. That's all I ask."

Twisting, I press a kiss to his crown. Hug him closer to my side. Bask in the revelations of the day. "Wish granted."

The hardest thing I have done is ask for help. It isn't a matter of pride. More my penchant for perfection.

But the Monday following my return from California, help is exactly what I started scavenging for.

I walked into the office and dove headfirst into work. Financials and emails and travel plans hadn't been at the top of my list as per usual. Instead, I made several calls to friends in my network. Calls I never thought I would make, but I knew it was time.

If I wanted a future with Reese, I needed to take this step. So I did.

Glancing at the time on my laptop, I wrap up an email to Centro Collective's local event coordinator. Bernadette has spent the last month preparing for our seventh-anniversary party. Each year, the festivities grow more grandiose. Decadent food, lavish drinks, live music, and memories our guests will share for years to come. Tickets to the event sell out in hours. The celebration ranked by several media outlets as *one party you don't want to miss*.

As I click send on the email, my phone intercom buzzes. "Mr. Callahan?"

"Yes, Dale?"

"Ms. Prescott is here for your two o'clock, sir."

"Please bring her back. Thank you, Dale."

The intercom disconnects and I take a deep breath. Work to calm the jitters beneath my diaphragm. Wipe my damp palms on my slacks. *When was the last time I was this nervous?*

You'd think it would have been when I realized my relationship with Reese was turning more serious. When we shifted from casual hookups to... more. But I never got jittery when it came to Reese and how I cared for him. For some inexplicable reason, I never broke a sweat at Reese and the possibility of a serious future together. Our relationship discovered a stronger foothold as of recent, but I never doubted how he felt. Now and again, I worried if we would last. Worried if my career would rip us apart. But each time I was hit with uncertainty, I quashed it. I never let the restlessness take hold.

Unlike now.

Maybe because Centro Collective is, for lack of a better term, my child. And what parent easily finds an adequate and respectable *stepparent* for their baby? Isn't that what this meeting is — an interview to find the right *co-parent* for my *child*?

Knocking sounds as Dale raps his knuckles on the

doorframe. "Ready, sir?" I bite my tongue not to laugh at Dale calling me sir.

As CEO of Centro Collective—nationally known as Callahan Industries Inc—I have heard the rumors. That I am a stuffed shirt and drill sergeant to my employees. Of course, the people that spread such fallacies have never worked for or with me or stepped foot in any of my buildings. They are also the same people that call me a daddy's boy. That whisper how I didn't work for what I have, that my father must be a silent partner or major financial contributor.

None of the rumors are true. Those who have stood by me since the beginning know the truth. Dale is one of those people, and he most definitely does not call me sir unless a new face is around.

"Yes, Dale. Thank you."

As he steps aside to let her enter, I fetch the folder from my credenza with Beverly Prescott's résumé. Hers is one of many I sifted through the past two days. A résumé detailed with prestigious business names and experience in all aspects of the companies. She'd climbed the ladder and had the accolades to prove it.

Pushing back, I rise from the chair, step around the desk, and offer my hand. "Ms. Prescott, I'm Trent Callahan. Pleasure to meet you." I gesture toward the love seat, chairs, and coffee table where I prefer to conduct in-person meetings. "Have a seat."

As we settle in, a wave of repose hits me without warning. Something about this woman puts me at ease. Perhaps it is her maternal vibe. Or the fact she has worked in businesses similar to mine for more than twenty years. Whatever it is, my anxiety from minutes ago evaporates.

This is what I need. This is how I better my relationship with Reese. By taking back my time.

I pluck the pen from inside my suit jacket and open the folder with her résumé. "Tell me a little about yourself, Ms. Prescott."

TRENT

Celebration is in order.

REESE

I won't say no. What are we celebrating?

For the first time since starting Centro Collective, I leave work on time. Well, on time for me. While most people work eight-hour days, I typically work ten to twelve, if not more. And weekends… what are those?

But after a lengthy interview and chat with Beverly Prescott, I made her an offer. What I didn't expect was for her to accept the offer before exiting my office. Not a minute after her departure, I called human resources, and Beth Anne pulled up the necessary paperwork.

In a blink, I'd hired an assistant. Well, Beverly would be more than an assistant—more like my counterpart, my right-hand woman. Not only would she take on the bulk of the paperwork I disliked, but she would also share some of the travel load. Similar to a COO, but with less overall company control. Beverly will help ensure Centro Collective runs without hiccups. Yes, I would have my hands in all things while she acclimates, but knowing I would no longer be attached at the hip to my job is a breath of fresh air.

TRENT

I hired my interviewee.

REESE

Definitely calls for drinks and dinner.

TRENT

Let me take you out. A proper date.

Dots dance in the little gray bubble then disappear. This happens again and again as I wait for his response. I bite the inside of my bottom lip as his message comes through.

REESE

Like flowers and candles and a romantic table for two?

My lips curve up in a smile. In two weeks, Reese and I will celebrate one year together. Though our relationship has felt on and off during the past twelve months, neither of us stepped out. During the weeks apart, when I "broke up" with Reese, we had the opportunity to be unfaithful. We remained loyal.

But I have never taken him on a date. A *real* date. Sure, we have attended events at Centro Collective together. Occasionally had drinks with his friends or grabbed a quick bite at a restaurant. I wouldn't classify those as dates, though. Not romantic dates.

Now that I will have more personal time, I plan to court and date the hell out of Reese Triggs.

TRENT

Possibly. Be ready in an hour. I'll pick you up.

REESE

I love it when you're bossy 😏

TRENT

Don't I know it.

Tapping the phone icon, I call a friend and cash in on a favor. Less than five minutes later, I pocket my phone, grab my keys, exit the office and lock up for the day.

As I slip behind the wheel of my car, happiness stings my cheeks. A delight I gladly accept, so long as Reese is the reason. So long as he is at my side.

FIVE

REESE

I TOSS MY PHONE ON THE BED AND DART TO THE bathroom.

One hour. That man only gave me one hour to get ready. Who does that? Trent Callahan, of course.

Cranking the hot water in the shower, I strip and dash under the spray. Wet my hair and lather it with shampoo. Rinse, then repeat the same steps with the conditioner. I load the loofah with body wash and do a thorough scrub down. As the last of the suds swirl down the drain, I shut off the water and step out to towel off.

After some quick manscaping, I head for the closet in search of clothes.

Trent gave no clues as to where he plans to take me for dinner. Knowing him, though, it won't be the mom-and-pop Italian joint up the street. No, Trent Callahan will wine and dine me tonight.

I pluck black slacks and a charcoal button-down from hangers. After slipping them on, I head back to the bathroom to add product to my curls and splash on the cologne that makes Trent ravenous. With one final look in the mirror, I exit the bathroom, grab socks and shoes, and head for the living room.

Days ago, the apartment was unrecognizable. Literal garbage and sweat-drenched clothes blanketed every surface. The smell was wretched, but I'd somehow become immune in my wallowing. And since no one else has set foot in here since Peyton moved out, I had zero concerns over the appearance or funk.

Until Trent and I talked and mended things.

The next day, I'd woken up hours before my shift at the rec center. Filled trash bags with days' worth of debris. Loaded the washer with a mountain of laundry. When I got home from the rec center, I continued my cleaning frenzy until it was time for my shift at the restaurant. I sprayed and wiped every table and countertop. Dusted and vacuumed and mopped. Sanitized the hell out of every room. Tossed the wet clothes in the dryer. And before I left for job two, I felt ten times better. The embarrassment over my living space dwindled.

Trent and I spent most of the weekend together. When we weren't cuddled on the couch, strolling along the beach surf or in bed, making up for lost time, we were at work. He at the Collective and me at the restaurant or home cleaning.

Parking on the couch, I get to work on my socks and shoes. A knock echoes through the apartment. Rising from the couch, I stumble as I wiggle my foot into the second shoe on the way to the door.

"Damnit," I mutter as I almost face-plant on the floor.

Righting myself, I walk a little slower to the door. *Like a nervous preteen all over again.* I disengage the lock, twist the handle, and open the door. At the sight of Trent, my skin heats as a massive smile stretches my face.

The man bought me flowers. Fucking. Flowers.

Swoon.

"Hi," I choke out then clear my throat. I open the door wider and step back. "Come in."

One step, then another, Trent leans forward and presses his lips to mine. "Hey." The three-letter word comes out raspy. He holds up the colossal bundle of red roses in brown paper. "Should put these in something before we go."

Can't believe he bought me flowers.

I had been joking when I texted him about flowers and candles. Should have known better.

Rummaging through the kitchen cabinets, I find an old vase buried in the back of one. Peyton must have forgotten it when she packed.

I fill the vase halfway with water and bring it to the counter where Trent unties the bouquet. After sprinkling in the flower food packet, he shoves the whole bouquet in the water. He fluffs out a few stems then smiles, obviously proud of himself.

"I love them," I admit quietly.

He turns to face me and takes a step closer. Inches apart, his warm, minty breath paints my lips. He lifts a hand and cups my cheek. "I love you." His eyes close for a beat. "God… never thought I'd say that to anyone other than family."

Leaning forward, I close the space between us and press my lips to his. The kiss is sweet and tender for one, two, three breaths. And then the energy between us shifts. Grows hungry. Wild. His tongue swipes my bottom lip before he sucks it between both of his. My hands go to his hips and haul him forward, my fingers bruising his flesh beneath the wool. Our tongues tangle and taste and beg for more.

And all too soon, he breaks the kiss. A groan rumbles in my chest and he chuckles at my obvious objection.

"We'll have time for more later." He drops a chaste kiss to my lips then inches away. "Don't want to miss our reservation."

"I'd rather stay in and have you for dinner," I tease.

"Another night." He takes my hand in his and walks backward toward the door. "I've never truly dated. Let me date the hell out of you. Dinners and movies and romantic walks under the full moon. Let me court you, love you." The last two words come out a touch softer.

As we reach the table in the foyer, I pocket my keys, wallet, and phone. I give a slight nod as we step out into the warm evening air. "Alright. Show me what you got, Callahan."

From the beginning, before Trent and I got to the *let's share more about ourselves* phase, I knew he was affluent. Not because he told me as much or I was up to date on who was wealthy in the area.

Trent radiates prestige. In the way he carries himself, in his choice of attire and how he speaks. Hell, the man owns an influential business and travels at least once a month for work.

But I have never taken stock in *how* wealthy Trent is. His money isn't why I love him.

In this place, a restaurant with napkins that probably cost more than my attire, I shrink inside myself. Crumple under judgmental eyes. Grow nauseous as I read the prices on the menu. *I don't belong here.* The words bounce around in my skull as I scan the restaurant for the third time.

Dim lighting from opulent chandeliers overhead. A single, lit white candle and red rose in a narrow, cylindrical vase at the heart of each black cloth-covered table. Each place setting with more plates and cutlery than I use in two meals. A wine menu as long as the book I recently read... with no prices listed.

Perspiration dampens my temples, my forehead, the back of my neck. The words on the menu go blurry as I stare at the price of the appetizers. *That is more than I make in an hour. Jesus.* Covertly, I glance over my menu and across the table to Trent, who appears completely unfazed by the dainty menu items and prices that could fill a cart of groceries.

"Anything catch your eye?" Trent asks as he lays his menu off to the side.

I swallow down the desire to scold him for bringing me here, to a place I don't belong. Voicing such opinions will only serve to upset us both. The last thing I want is to spark another argument. If I want to be with Trent, I need to change my perception of his lifestyle. Trent is more than a beautiful face and brilliant mind. He also wields power.

Awkward as it may be to adjust to this reality, this side of him, in order for us to have a future, I need to be willing to bend and flex with him. Dine at the ritzy restaurants and wear the nice clothes as I lock arms with him at events. It won't be an everyday occurrence, but it will happen often enough to be considered normal.

Pushing past my natural inclination to veto every item due to the price tag, I inhale deeply and say, "Can't decide if I want fish or steak."

"Had my eye on the New York Strip. Get the fish and we can share."

I nod, picking up my water and downing half the glass. "Sounds like a plan."

The server returns and takes our respective orders, not writing anything down. Trent adds the artisanal cheese appetizer to the order as well as a bottle of cabernet sauvignon.

Dark-green irises lock me in place the moment the server steps away. His fingers twist the stem of the water glass back and forth, back and forth, as his head tips slightly to the side. Wordlessly, he regards me for a beat. Studies me as my brows twitch on occasion and I bite the inside of my cheek. His scrutiny doesn't add to my anxiety or make me uncomfortable. If anything, it has me curious about how much he sees when his eyes take me in.

"You're uneasy," he states. Since he didn't pose it as a question, I don't respond. One corner of his mouth kicks up. "But not with me."

I shake my head. As I open my mouth to tell him he is partially correct, the server returns to the table with the wine and two glasses. Setting the glasses down, he uncorks the bottle, pours a small amount into one glass, and offers it to Trent.

Mesmerized, I watch as Trent swirls the wine in the glass before bringing it to his nose and inhaling deeply. He shifts the rim of the glass to his lips, tips back, and takes a small sip. Two breaths pass before he swallows and nods. The server fills both glasses, places the bottle on the table, then disappears.

Needing something to settle my nerves, I scoop up the glass and guzzle half the contents. Trent doesn't say a word, but I see the smirk on his lips behind his own glass.

"Uneasy isn't the right word," I finally say. "More like overwhelmed. This"—I gesture around the room with my chin—"is a lot to take in."

He gives a slight nod. "At times, it is for me too." His eyes latch on mine as he grants me his devilishly handsome half smile. "Believe it or not, this isn't my scene most of the time. Sure, I know a thing or two about quality and what I like, but most of that stems from my upbringing." Leaning forward, he braces his elbows on the table and clasps his fingers in front of his mouth. "My scene is more like where we met."

Flashes of that night, almost a year ago, play in my memory. The gay nightclub in Tampa. Too many drinks. Dancing and sweating and gyrating against him for hours. His lips on mine in the middle of the dance floor. The drive back to my place. Lips and tongues and teeth on skin. The way he moaned my name and fisted my hair.

Damn, that was a great night.

"We should go there again," I say, heat crawling up my neck and cheeks.

"Mmm, I agree." He sips his wine. "Another night, though. We already have plans tonight."

"We do?"

"Yes."

Over the next hour, I focus on Trent and push away the luxury bleeding from the walls. He tells me about the woman he hired today and how that will alleviate a hefty amount of his workload and travel. I tell him about the sixtysomething that wouldn't stop flirting at the rec center pool today. We talk and laugh and enjoy our first legit date.

When the server delivers the bill, I sip my water and think about anything other than money. Minutes later, we are in the car and on the road.

We drive a few miles down Gulf Boulevard before Trent flips the blinker and turns onto a cobblestone driveway. Before I can ask where we are, he rolls down his window and punches in a code to access the gated drive. I stop breathing as the car stops in front of a million-dollar house. The sheer size of it swallows me whole.

This is his *house.* I swallow. Try to remember how to breathe. *This man is worth more at thirty-six than I will earn in my lifetime.*

I don't deserve him. And he deserves much more than the likes of me.

SIX

TRENT

Bringing him here without warning was foolish. I see it in the glazed-over look in his eyes.

Fuck. What was I thinking?

My hand hovers over the keypad to unlock the front door. "We can leave," I blurt out as my hand falls to my side. "If this is too much."

He reaches for and takes my hand, giving it a squeeze. "No." His eyes shift from me to the front door. "It's just… a lot, and all in one night." Soft laughter leaves his lips. "It's been almost a year and I'm just now seeing this side of you. I knew it existed." He shrugs. "Guess I compartmentalized it all."

Makes sense. It hadn't been my intention to wait this long to bring Reese to my home. Between my work schedule and wanting time with him, it had been easier to stay at his place. But it was time for that to change.

In the past, I'd never brought men home. My father taught me at a young age to be leery of outsiders. *"Learn who they really are before they step foot in your home."* I'd thought he was paranoid… until one of his newer employees got caught stuffing Mom's jewelry in his pocket. One occurrence was all it took for Dad to never host parties at the house again.

Reese has never given me reason to mistrust him — not in life or love — which is why I feel safe opening my home to him. But I didn't consider how he would take in the magnitude of my life. It is no secret to him that I have money. Tonight just happens to be the first time I *flaunt* said money.

"Promise me something."

He narrows his eyes for a breath. "Okay," he drawls out the word.

"If you want to leave, at any time, you'll tell me."

Leaning forward, he presses a gentle kiss to my lips. I don't miss the slight tremble in his touch. "Promise."

Entering the code, I unlock the front door and walk us inside. I disengage the alarm and flip on the light in the foyer. Much as I want to show off my house and give Reese a tour, I don't want to add fuel to the *too much in one night* fire.

His fingers threaded with mine, I steer us toward the kitchen. As we step into the room, lights under the cabinets come to life and glow softly in the darkness. Beside me, Reese stiffens, but I continue forward.

"Nightcap?" I ask as I twist to face him.

He nods. "Yeah, sure."

Releasing my hold on him, I go to the bar area of the kitchen, turn over two tumblers, and pour bourbon into the glasses. He watches my every move until I hand him a drink, his eyes dropping to the glass as he brings it to his lips. I wait for his reaction as he sips the sweet, earthy liquor.

His Adam's apple bobs. "Smooth," he whispers.

I down the contents of my glass then set both of ours on the counter. "It is."

In the next breath, I take his hand and walk us through the house. A slow trek up the stairs, down the north hall and into the bedroom suite. The moment we pass the threshold, my skin buzzes and body hums.

No one has felt this right.

"Take off my clothes, Reese." I drop his hand, spin to face him, and walk backward into the room. "Stake your claim. On me. In my home. In my bed."

His apprehension from moments ago morphs into fire. He toes off his shoes and kicks them aside but makes no move to strip his own clothes. Like a hunter stalking prey, he saunters in my direction.

Hypnotized by his gaze, I swallow when his tongue darts out to lick his lips. A hand reaches for my belt, unlatching the buckle and whipping it from the loops. Dexterous fingers tug at the base of my dress shirt, pulling the tails from my slacks before popping each button and shoving the material down my arms.

Inches from my skin, his breath is hot and hungry as he slowly strips me bare. But he doesn't touch my exposed flesh. Not yet. Our labored breaths echo in the room as my slacks puddle at my feet. I kick them to the side and pant as I wait for what Reese will do next.

Before I conjure the countless ways he might take me, he drops to his knees and stares up at me as if I am a god. His hands take my hips, knead my flesh for two breaths, then slowly peel my briefs down.

I cup his cheek as my cock stands proudly before him. "Take what's yours, Reese. What will always be yours."

Eyes on mine, his calloused fingers trail up my thighs and around my hips until they dig into the muscles of my ass and haul me forward. And before I can take a breath, the heat of his mouth wraps around my length.

Fuck.

The scent of sex mixed with Reese's cologne fills my nose as I wake. Darkness blankets the room and I don't know if it's because the sun hasn't risen or the curtains block it out.

Either way, I don't care. Reese is in my arms, his back to my front, and there is nowhere else I want to be.

My eyes drift closed as I inhale the smell of him. Let it soothe my soul and give me life. Reese has always done that, provided comfort and brightened my world. Since day one, he wrapped me up and never let go. Not that I would want him to.

Without thinking, I kiss the back of his neck. Tighten my hold on him.

A groan rumbles in his chest before he rubs his ass against my now-thickening erection. "Naptime over?" He laces his fingers with mine and rocks against me once more. "Mmm. Definitely over."

Before I get a word in, he guides my hand down his chest, his abdomen, to the junction of his thighs, where his cock is hot and thick and waiting. I kiss the back of his neck again, this time with tongue and teeth, as I wrap my fingers around his cock.

"So fucking perfect," I growl in his ear.

Reaching behind, he palms the back of my head and holds me to him. I pump his cock in slow, measured strokes with a slight pinch when I reach the tip. Just how he loves it. His other hand fists the sheet as I stroke myself between his ass cheeks.

His cock thickens further in my hand, and I know he is close. I rock my hips faster while keeping the same pace with his cock. A deep, guttural moan fills the air and I bite down where his shoulder and neck meet. He comes on the next stroke up, and I follow, our orgasms painting the sheets and our flesh.

And before either of us comes down from our high, I blurt out, "Move in with me."

Reese freezes, and the air turns to ice.

Fuck.

SEVEN

REESE

Heat of the moment or legitimate question?

After a year together, Trent asking me to move in isn't outrageous. But midorgasm…

Did he actually mean to ask?

Not giving a damn about the sheets or the mess, I roll over until we are face to face. *I need to see him.* Though the room is dark, my eyes immediately find his. Hope glints in his eyes while fear tugs at his brows.

"Are you serious?" I ask, keeping my voice as level as possible. "Or was that a slip?"

His hand comes to my cheek as he leans in and kisses my lips. "I didn't mean for it to come out like that, or during sex, but yes…" The soft skin of his thumb caresses my stubble. "I love you, Reese. I want to be with you. Share my life with you. Exist in the same space." His eyes dart between mine. "Move in with me," he whispers.

I digest his words. As much as I would love to scream *yes*, this should be something I give more consideration.

"It's not a no, but can I think on it?"

I don't miss the slight flinch in his expression, but it is probably because he isn't used to waiting for answers. "Yes. Of course." He glances at the clock on the side table. "It's early. Let's shower and have breakfast before I drive you home."

And just like that, it feels as if the topic never came up. *Ugh.*

We shower in silence and without any attempts at teasing or tasting. Although he says to leave them, I strip the sheets while he heads downstairs to make breakfast. *I just need a minute to think.*

As I tug the linens free, I give the idea of living with Trent merit. Of living in this monstrosity of a house. Transitioning from minuscule to immeasurable. Taking this step with him is huge. Just as momentous as us exchanging I love yous.

Can I do this? Coexist with him in this world every day?

By the time I reach the bottom floor, Trent has scrambled eggs, bacon, and buttered toast on plates. Silence clouds around us as we eat and get ready to leave. A silence more deafening than the loudest sound. I hate everything about this silence. It is a punishment. A punishment I don't deserve.

As we pull out of the driveway, I swallow past every ounce of fear. Reaching over the console, I take his hand and thread our fingers. Stare at our joined hands. "You know I love you, right?"

"Why do I not like the start of this conversation?" he asks, emotion thick in his voice.

I risk a glance at his profile and see him swallow. "I love you. I'm *in* love with you."

His eyes leave the road for a split second and flash in my direction. "I love you too." Warm fingers reinforce their hold on my hand.

"I want to say yes."

We reach a red light and he twists to regard me. "Then say yes." A horn honks and he groans before facing forward to drive.

I swallow past the truth lump thickening in my throat. "What if living together isn't what we expect? You're busy running an empire and I work two jobs to make ends meet." He opens his mouth to cut in and I hold up a hand. "And before you tell me I don't need to work, not happening."

Steering the car into the apartment complex, he remains quiet as he parks beside my car. He cuts the engine but doesn't make a move otherwise. He simply stares out the windshield. Several breaths pass before he shrugs and turns to meet my panicky gaze.

"I'm pretty optimistic. In most things. And this, us" — he gestures between us — "I am damn confident will work out."

"Damn confident, huh?" He nods and I continue. "So what happens when I complain about your hours and not giving me what I need?"

His lips kick up into that devilish smile I can't resist. The smile that lured me in. "Then I work less or take you with me on trips. As far as giving you what you need..." He leans over the console and crooks his finger. Leaning in, I leave a breath between us. "Reese Triggs, I will *always* give you what you need." With that, he crushes my lips with his.

When the kiss breaks, I feel dizzy. Not just from his lips on mine but also because I am about to change everything. I am about to leap. Change us forever.

"Then I say yes," I whisper.

As long as Trent is by my side, as long as he loves me, the answer will always be yes.

EIGHT

TRENT

Too much is happening all at once. Major changes at work with the addition of Beverly Prescott. Even bigger changes in my personal life as Reese slowly packs up his apartment and prepares to move into my house. I welcome change, but to have two major life events simultaneously… my ribs constrict and shorten my breaths.

In the past month, Beverly Prescott has learned a lot about Callahan Industries. More than any other person. With the exception of me, naturally.

Each morning, her heels clap the polished concrete floor as she enters her office. The office next to mine. She stows her purse and swanky tote, brews a cup of coffee in her aqua-colored Keurig, then walks into my office with the cinnamon roll-scented beverage, pen and paper. On Mondays, we discuss the week's schedule and any changes. What meetings I will attend and the ones on her roster. Trips out of state and which of us will go. And that is just Monday.

Tuesday through Friday is… exhausting.

For someone with a stellar résumé and jaw-dropping accolades, Beverly Prescott needs a lot of assistance and attention. Time was something she was to grant me, not take away.

Overall, the addition of her position has been good. Hiccups were something I expected, as well as the unease of bringing in an unfamiliar face and sharing my role. Any person in my shoes would be uncomfortable handing over a key to the kingdom. I built this company from the ground up. Have invested millions of dollars and countless hours. Letting go, even just a little, is difficult.

New employee and expected hiccups aside, something is *off*.

Relinquishing smaller tasks has been easier. Ms. Prescott is now a major point of contact within the company. She checks in with construction managers at the sites being built then reports back with details. Anything requiring an executive decision still comes to my desk. It is too soon to allow her that level of power. She also reaches out to the general managers at each location. Discusses day-to-day business and concerns. Offers solutions to drive revenue.

Also on her list of responsibilities is data collection from each Centro Collective location. She enters the details into spreadsheets for weekly review by yours truly. Eventually, the task will involve cross-checking the data with sums on invoices and statements.

The majority of the jobs I've doled out are monotonous. Figures and number crunching, paperwork and general tasks most would handle without assistance. Basic administrative work I'd expect someone with a lesser skill set to accomplish effortlessly.

Giving up bigger components of the job has been stressful. Allowing her to fly in my stead to different locales and touch base with each Centro Collective crew in person—which has only happened once to Orlando. Talking with the managers and staff and being an integral part of the company I spent years establishing.

I get that not many CEOs visit every branch of their company. I get that they don't immerse themselves in the day-to-day tasks that can be delegated to someone else. But I am not like every other business owner.

Being involved, in some fashion, with every facet of my business is vital. This company is my name, my lifeblood, my future. How will I recognize problems within the company walls if I am clueless about the standard operation?

I don't *need* to do it all, but relinquishing parts of my job twists a knife in my gut.

"Morning, Mr. Callahan," Beverly singsongs as she waltzes into my office with her confection-scented beverage. A smile on her pink-painted lips as she reaches the chair. She sets her coffee and notepad on the table then takes a seat.

"Good morning, Ms. Prescott."

Unlike everyone else in the office, I still address Beverly Prescott formally. Those not in my inner circle would call me an asshole for still using formalities with her, but I don't care what others think. Not when it comes to *my* business. Informal titles are earned with time and trust and evidence you will stay long term.

One month is nowhere near enough time for any staff member to earn my trust or easygoing persona. If the queasiness over the past week is any indication, trust will be a challenge with this woman.

Trust your intuition. It hasn't failed you yet.

Can't quite put my finger on it, but something is not aboveboard with Beverly Prescott. Her sunny disposition and penchant for long hours seem too… perfect. Now and then, I question the sincerity of her smile and high-pitched greetings. I analyze her eagerness to stay late at the office, later than everyone else. More than anything, it is the random questions she asks out of nowhere. Questions that dig a little too deep into Callahan Industries. And questions too personal for someone speaking with her new boss.

I collect the tablet from my desk and meet her at the circle of seats. "What updates do you have for me?"

She flips through a few pages of her notepad and I grind my jaw to keep from huffing in frustration. I drum my fingers as I wait for her to locate her current notes. The longer she fumbles, the more my blood heats.

"Raul from the Chicago store —"

"Location," I cut her off, the word blade sharp as it leaves my lips.

"Yes, Mr. Callahan." She clears her throat, takes a sip

of her coffee, then continues. "Raul from the Chicago location says all the spaces have been rented and there is now a waiting list for openings."

Expansion of specific Centro Collective locations has been brewing for several months. Waiting lists equal demand. And demand means it is time to move forward with add-ons.

"What else?" I tap on the notes app on my tablet and type *speak with Raul*.

She shuffles through the scribbled pages of her notepad again and I growl internally. Scanning the next page, she stops. "Nothing else to report this week." A white, toothy smile spreads wide on her face.

"Nothing?" I deadpan as I set down my tablet.

She shakes her head, her smile falling as she takes in my clenched jaw and obvious irritation.

"Ms. Prescott, what job am I paying you to do?" I bite out. I don't ask the question to get an actual answer. So when she opens her mouth to speak, I hold up my hand. "I know what you are being paid to do." My lips purse as I cross my arms over my chest. "Hell, I created the job. Wrote the damn job description myself."

"I-I—"

"Dale is my personal assistant, Ms. Prescott. I don't need another. What I *do* need is someone to pick up the excess. Someone to act in my stead when I cannot attend a meeting or travel or spend all night in the office. I need someone competent and not just pretty on paper." With each word, my voice escalates. Takes on an acerbic edge.

"Someone organized, that can multitask and answer a damn question in regard to my business without fumbling."

Her glassy eyes widen as she fidgets in her chair; my blunt nature not something she is accustomed to. Until now, I have coddled her. Let her dysfunctionality slide.

But the time for games is over. I hired her because she was the best of all the candidates. Her résumé was gold. Speech articulate and professional. Appearance sharp and polished. She walked into the interview and delivered everything I was looking for. She wowed me with promises. Held her own.

That Beverly was a ruse. And if there is one thing I despise, it is dishonesty.

I will not be played the fool.

I rise from the chair, walk back to my desk, and rest my hands on the surface. After two breaths, I meet her gaze. "You have two weeks to prove you can do the job as described, Ms. Prescott." I straighten my spine and square my shoulders. "If I deem you incapable of the role, I have no choice but to let you go." I sit in my desk chair and wake my computer up. "You can go," I dismiss her without looking in her direction.

In my periphery, she gathers her belongings, hugs them to her chest, and shuffles out of the office. When the soft click of the office door closing sounds, I deflate in my seat.

"Fuck," I whisper, dropping my head in my hands.

When something appears too good to be true, it most

likely is. And fuck my life, because Beverly Prescott came across as the perfect person to be my right hand.

Now, I am not so sure. Now, I have more work to do.

"Sorry, Reese. If it were up to me, I wouldn't fire anyone." Jake props his hands on his hips and looks to the side. He purses his lips and huffs out a breath. "Not that it'll make you feel better, but it looks like the owner is selling or declaring bankruptcy. Better to get out now."

Is there a great way to lose your job? No, never.

Hell, I could be a server at one of the thousands of restaurants in the Bay Area. Could make bank at plenty of the flashy places on the water or in the ritzy hotels. Stockpile my savings and pay off my car loan a year earlier. But I chose to stay at this family-owned, twenty-four-hour diner because I love the people—customers and coworkers. They are family. People who share their life stories with me and vice versa.

Being fired... I'm gutted. Like my family got ripped away.

I clap Jake on the shoulder and plaster on an artificial smile. "Just doing your job, man. Really hope they don't sell. Would be a shame to lose what they worked so hard to build."

"Agreed." He reaches for and takes my hand. "Been a pleasure working with you, Reese. We'll mail the final pay stub."

I drop his hand and take one last look around the open storeroom. Large cans of vegetables and fruits and crushed tomatoes line the bottom shelves. Rice and dried beans and pasta on the shelves above. As my eyes climb, my vision blurs. *I hate this.*

"Actually, will you call me and hold it? With the move, I don't want it lost in the mail."

He cups the back of his neck and squeezes. "Shit, how did I forget that was coming up? You ready?"

With a shake of my head, I chuckle. "Is anyone ever ready to move?" I untie my apron and toss it in the bin. "Everything but necessities are packed. The heavy lifting happens this weekend."

Discomfiture rolls over me like an incoming tide, a sense I no longer belong here, and I hate how much I want to bolt for the door. Run from a place I've always felt welcome, at home. Jake says it isn't personal, that several others will suffer the same fate, but damn, it stings. Like a parent slapping you across the face, then crying because they hurt you.

Nausea hits out of nowhere. Sweat slicks the back of my neck. I take a deep breath, beg the bile to stay down, then swallow. *I need out of here.*

I take a step toward the back door, lift a hand and wave. "See you in a couple weeks."

A sad smile dons his face. *Slap.* "Yeah. See you."

I exit through the back, unlock my car, and slip behind the wheel. I crank the engine and air conditioning, my knuckles pale as I grip the steering wheel. A thump ricochets in my head as it smacks the wheel between my hands.

Concerned as I was about moving in with Trent, thank goodness I am. Better to have decided because we want to live together rather than out of necessity.

Without the restaurant job, I'd be royally fucked living in the apartment on my own. Thank goodness I had the sense to stash money away when Peyton and I were roomies. Little by little, I padded my savings account. Put enough away to pay bills for a few months in case anything went south.

Losing my job sucks, but it came at a time when I don't have to worry as much.

I straighten in my seat and suck in a deep breath. Stare at the faded blue paint on the restaurant wall. Say one last goodbye, then throw the car in reverse, back out, and aim the car toward home. Well, what will be my home for a few more days.

"One week," I mutter to myself. "Then go out and find a new damn job."

I set down my chopsticks and rub my stomach. "Damn, I needed that."

Trent laughs as he lifts a brown bottle to his lips. "You and me both."

Reaching across the table, I take his hand. Bat my lashes and smile. "Tell me about your day, dear."

He snorts. "Please, don't call me *dear*. Sounds like something Nana L would say."

"Nana L?"

"Lucille, my father's mom. Sweetest person you'll ever meet. The type of grandmother that squeezes cheeks then gives sloppy kisses on said cheeks." A softness settles over Trent's features. An unspoken fondness for his grandmother. Someone I hope to meet, along with the rest of his family, in the future.

I have never met *the parents* with anyone. Not having a serious relationship before Trent, I never went through any of the "normal" phases of a relationship. No schmoozing over dinner at a nice restaurant. No heavy topics of discussion. Definitely no cohabitation. And never the chance to meet relatives.

Until now, meeting extended family held no appeal. Until Trent, sex was all I wanted from someone.

"I look forward to meeting her," I say. "But seriously, how was your day?" Can't be worse than mine.

"Beverly Prescott is walking a fine line." He takes a long pull from his beer and sighs. "Had such high hopes for her." He peels the label back on his bottle. "She wowed me with her résumé. Intrigued me during her interview. But now… I didn't expect her to be so lacking."

Rising from my seat, I tug Trent's hand and walk us to the couch.

In two days, all the large furniture will be picked up by a local charity that helps low-income households—singles and families alike—that desperately need furnishings but can't afford the steep prices in retail stores. The dining room table with four chairs will be sold for fifty dollars. The couch for twenty. Households add their name to a waiting list after financial proof of hardship. They check off what they need and get notified when an item becomes available.

If I knew the people firsthand, I'd gift them the furniture for free. But I understand the need or desire for anonymity. People don't want to be judged—not that I would judge them—and prefer to keep their financial woes as private as possible.

"Lacking in what way?"

Trent tips his head, resting it on the back of the couch. He rocks his head left, then right, then stops when he hits center. "With her supposed level of experience and expertise, I shouldn't have to hold her hand"—he tilts his head to look at me—"every damn day. Figuratively, but still."

I wince. "You raved over her credentials. From everything you shared, she sounded perfect for the job. Sorry things aren't what they seemed."

He lifts a hand from his lap and traces the design on my graphic tee. "Me too." His hand falls to my thigh and clamps the muscle. "Please tell me your day was better."

I purse my lips and slowly shake my head. "Define better."

Lifting his head, he twists in his seat to face me, his hand taking mine. "What happened?"

"The restaurant isn't doing well financially." I shrug and drop my gaze to our joined hands, my thumb stroking his soft skin. "And I was let go."

The words are barely out when Trent pinches my chin between his thumb and forefinger, lifting until I meet his gaze. I expect to see excitement or relief or some awkward version of happiness that I no longer work at what Trent may deem an unnecessary job. But none of those emotions color his expression.

Instead, an edge of sadness turns down the corners of his mouth. Softens his evergreen irises. Has him leaning closer.

It makes me love him that much more.

"That fucking sucks."

"Yeah. It does." I twist and kiss his palm. "But I still have the rec center. And after the move, I'll start looking for something else."

Trent opens his mouth. Words try to shape his lips but fail.

I don't want to fight. Not tonight. Not after things have been going smoothly the past month. Arguments, or the thought of one, make me nauseous. Make me want to curl in on myself. Healthy debate? Cool. I have no issue expressing my point of view in a calm manner and listening to someone do the same, followed by finding middle ground. But spewing hurtful words at loud volumes with grotesque expressions... no one forgets those moments.

Right now, I need my boyfriend to hold me. To tell me

it will all work out. That I will find a job I love more than the previous. To encourage and cheer me on.

As if he hears my thoughts, he tugs me into his side, wraps an arm around my shoulders, and kisses my temple. I drop my head to his shoulder and snake an arm around his waist. My eyes fall shut as his thumb paints small circles on my bicep.

"Do you want another hospitality job?" he whisper-asks.

I give a halfhearted shrug. "It's what I know, so probably."

A hum vibrates his throat before he rests his head on mine. "Crazy ideas are crowding my thoughts."

I open my eyes as my fingertip traces the rim of the button on his dress shirt, one lazy circle after another. "Crazy how?"

Trent goes momentarily silent. His thumb continues to stroke my arm, rhythmic and gentle. Without interruption, I grant him time to declutter his thoughts. Organize them before he speaks up.

And while he thinks, I relax and focus on all things him. The clean, crisp scent of his starched button-down mixed with the sweet bergamot cedar smell of his cologne. The warmth of his skin through the fabric of his shirt. The rise and fall of his chest with each steady breath. The buzz along my skin as his hand drifts over my shoulder, up the back of my neck, and into my curls.

"Would you be open to trying something new?" he asks as his fingers massage my scalp with soft strokes.

I haven't put thought into looking at jobs outside of

hospitality. When you've worked in the same industry your entire adult life, you gravitate toward what you know. On the beach, especially near Trent's house—our house—hourly pay and tips are the best in the county. Like all industries, hospitality folks talk. We meet in bars and chat about the good, bad, and disturbing. With any job, working in restaurants has its ups and downs. But the only way I see myself not serving tables is if the perfect opportunity strikes.

And I have no clue what said opportunity looks like.

"Depends on what it is. I wouldn't discount anything without knowing more."

Beside me, Trent grows oddly quiet again. Deepening the pressure, his fingers continue massaging my scalp and I hum at his soft but firm touch. *God, I love his hands on me.* Every brush of his skin on mine. Every dig or scratch or graze ignites undeniable heat. Makes me want him more. Makes me love him more.

His fingers drift to my neck, soft, lazy strokes lighting a fire under my skin.

"Would you work with me?" he whisper-asks.

My breath catches in my throat. My forehead tightening as my brows tug in and down. *Work with Trent?*

The idea doesn't repulse me, but I also know nothing about his job or business. Or what he would ask me to do if I said yes. Sitting at a desk all day, answering the phone and being an errand boy holds no appeal.

And isn't it a big relationship no-no to work with your significant other? I am by no means the morality police, but working with someone you are romantically involved with seems unethical. A one-way street to breakup town.

"Uh…"

I sit straighter and twist to face him. Read his expression and gauge if this is a serious proposal. Dark-green irises lock me in place. The corners of his mouth tip up, the action almost hidden by the scruff lining his jaw. Then I scan the line of his body, make note of his relaxed posture and widespread legs. His free hand rests on his thigh.

Has Trent ever looked this comfortable in his own skin? It isn't often we just get to be like this. Chill. Laid back. Between work schedules and the recent decision to move in together, downtime is a rarity.

"Maybe?" My answer comes out as a question. I need more details before giving a definitive answer.

His warm breath paints my lips as he chuckles. His hand is back in my hair, sweeping the curls from my face before his fingers trail my jawline. He leans in, presses a chaste kiss to my lips, and makes me melt.

"God, I love you."

Smiling wide, I fist his shirt and pull him in for a deeper kiss. "Love you too, T."

Seriousness replaces the soft lines of his expression. "I'll probably fire Beverly." His entire body deflates with a sigh. "I told her two weeks, and I will give her as much, but I don't think she's cut out for the job." Fingers dive into his hair and pull once before his palm slaps his thigh. "Ugh. I really hate being the boss sometimes," he teases.

"Liar." I wink at him.

He rolls his eyes. "At times like this, it sucks." The pad of his thumb strokes my cheek. Slow and steady. Back and forth. "Even if she shows major improvement, I don't think I'll keep her for the role. It's not worth the risk. Tomorrow, I'll check with human resources and see what other openings we have. Maybe we have something more her style in a different department."

At this, all the pieces lock in place. Trent doesn't just want me to work for his company, he wants me to be his second-in-command. The person who takes work off his plate so he has more time outside the office.

Again, I question how great this idea is.

Won't we get sick of each other? Argue and complain more?

Last thing I want is to become one of those couples that can't stand the sight of each other but continue forward in the hopes it will get better. That isn't love. That is coasting along.

But what if the complete opposite happens? What if we love working together? What if this experience opens up doors for us both? What if this job is something *I* love?

I initially thought it might be a desk job. Grunt work and mind-numbing boredom. But Trent wouldn't stick me in a job I'd tire of easily. He'd load up my schedule and surrender tasks he trusts in my hands.

"And you want me to take her place?" I ask, needing clarification before I get ahead of myself.

Subtly, he nods. "Yeah." His thumb drifts to my chin before brushing over my lips, his eyes following the action. "First off, you're brilliant. I know you love serving and lifeguard duty. If you want to do that, I'll understand. But I'm not oblivious to how organized you are. Even on your worst days, you know where everything is." He shrugs. "Learning paperwork and the scope of the job are basics. You'd have it down in days."

Inching back, I hold up a hand. Cock my head and narrow my eyes. "Listen to you. Talking like I said yes already."

"You will."

"And what if I don't?"

"You will."

Laughter spills from my lips. "Cocky much?"

The corner of his mouth kicks up. "Not cocky. Certain. There's a difference." He fists the collar of my T-shirt and tugs me to him. "One week. Think about it."

I lick my lips, swallow, and groan. "I fucking love it when you're bossy."

He crushes my mouth with his. Parts my lips with his tongue and fucks my mouth with his until we are both gasping for air.

Rising from the couch, he takes my hand and hauls me from the cushion. He laces our fingers, taking one step, then another. "Let's go to bed and you can show me how much you love my bossiness."

"Yes, sir, boss man."

Brow cocked, he smirks. "Yep. You most definitely will accept the job." He leads us down the hall and into my mostly bare bedroom. Spinning around, he unbuttons his shirt. "Now... fuck me like you mean it."

TEN

TRENT

TODAY IS IT. THE LAST STRAW. THE END OF THE LINE. And she is fucking late.

Not just a little late, as in she hit traffic or every red light on the way. A stickler for punctuality, I forgive circumstances beyond someone's control. But her tardiness is her own doing. The woman lives five miles from the office, traffic isn't a major issue of concern.

I shake my wrist and glance down at my watch. "Thirty-five fucking minutes," I grumble under my breath.

Several unsavory facts about Ms. Beverly Prescott have come to light in the past week. Facts that cannot be ignored.

I'd granted her two weeks. Two weeks to prove she could handle the job. Two weeks to demonstrate I didn't waste valuable resources, time, and money on someone incompetent.

A week and a half have passed, and I am done. Beyond done.

When we started the hiring process for this role, human resources did blanket checks of each applicant. Arrest records with a focus on felonies. Generic calls to the former employers listed on each résumé. Standard calls to listed references. During this process, no red flags popped up in regard to Beverly Prescott.

Once I voiced concerns to human resources—Beverly's blatant inability to perform the job and her overexuberance to be at the top—they made more calls. Reaching out to fellow human resources friends in the area and digging deeper. Like all lines of work, people working in the same circles talk. Beth Anne, the human resources director for Callahan Industries Inc., made calls and had lunch dates with industry friends in the area.

According to the human resources reps from the businesses on Beverly Prescott's résumé, she was a wolf in sheep's clothing. They had never been able to point the finger directly at her—she'd covered her tracks well—but financial records weren't matching the bank accounts. It started weeks after each new job. Beverly Prescott had funneled money from each business into untraceable accounts.

It started small at first. Pennies at a time out of large accounts she oversaw. She'd manipulated the books for years. Tweaked spreadsheets and "lost" bank statements. No one was able to point a finger directly at Beverly. No trails led solely to her. So no charges were pressed. She was fired and security precautions were taken.

And in her absence, the problem disappeared and the companies recovered.

When I asked Beth Anne about calls made to previous employers and references, she said receptionists or assistants handled the former employment calls. They answer basic questions and could be none the wiser to Beverly's indiscretions. When it comes to personal references, those are easier to manipulate. Anyone could be on the other end, ready to boast and highlight Beverly's false work ethic. Indisputably, Beverly's references are partners in her fraud scheme.

Unfortunately for Beverly Prescott, I don't fuck around. People who know me say I am cutthroat when it comes to business. I won't deny that truth.

When I started Callahan Industries, I wasn't in business to make friends. I was in business to fulfill opportunities, meet needs, and build a future. I didn't reach this point in my career with kind words and a lack of authority. Callahan Industries is what it is today because I spearheaded this company with an iron fist. I inserted myself in every part of the process. I approved each project and oversaw every penny spent. This company is more than dollar signs, it is my blood, sweat, and frustrations. It is a dream I worked my ass off to achieve. It holds the key to my future and livelihood.

And no one will smile to my face and rob me behind my back. No one. Especially a conniving twit like Beverly Prescott.

Winded, Beverly bounds into the office formerly deemed hers. "Oh." She slaps a hand to her chest. "So sorry I'm late, Mr. Callahan." She shrugs her purse higher and hugs it closer to her chest. Her eyes avert and spot the box on the desk. "Is everything alright?"

Arriving at the office before the sun rose or anyone clocked in, I plucked an empty storage box from the file room and started packing Beverly's belongings. Beth Anne collected the company laptop from the office a little more than an hour ago, taking it to technology security to be scrubbed for malware and searched for all past activity since given to Beverly.

I take a deep breath and audibly exhale as I push off the edge of the desk. "Ms. Prescott, it has come to our attention that you were dishonest during the hiring process."

"I don't know—"

Holding up a hand, I silence her. I don't need more of her lies. "It'd be best if you don't speak."

Swiping the box off the desk, I hold it out for her to take. Her eyes pinch for a split second as she eyes the box. The muscles in her jaw flex as her nostrils flare long enough for me to take notice. And then she straightens her spine and squares her shoulders. The corners of her mouth tip up in an unrepentant, false smile as she steps forward and takes the box.

"Please follow me."

I exit the office, stand in the hall, brush my hands down my suit jacket, and wait for her to follow. Head held high, she steps out of the office and distances herself. I close the door behind her and check the newly changed lock has engaged.

Without a word, I lead her down one hall, then

another, before we reach human resources. I open the door, step aside, and gesture for her to enter. Sneer firmly in place, she passes me and walks into the office. Beth Anne and Radford—the head of technology security for Callahan Industries Inc—stand poised in reception. I fight the chill that rolls over my skin as Beverly regards the present company.

"This is where we part ways, Ms. Prescott. Beth Anne will collect your keys and badge then answer any questions regarding your termination. All personal items are in the box," I state, pointing to the box in her hands. "All company property has been accounted for and you may leave when Beth Anne finishes speaking with you."

I shift my gaze to Beth Anne, give a tight smile and nod, then spin on my heel to leave.

Instantaneous relief relaxes my muscles as I walk back to my office.

If not for my meticulousness and apprehension, Beverly Prescott might have masterminded more schemes before anyone at Callahan Industries took notice. She had the tools and access to cause irrevocable damage. To steal millions and tear apart my business from the inside.

I mentally clap my hands in prayer and send a silent thank you to my father. In my years at Callahan Financial, I'd heard the whispers and break room gossip. Paranoid and ludicrous were words people used to describe Michael Callahan and his obsessive need to keep an eye on all aspects of his business. I saw it more as a defensive measure. Had he not instilled the same strong virtues in me, my business might have gone down the shitter.

"Bless your paranoia, Father," I mutter as I enter my office and shut the door.

Pushing the events of the morning out of my head, I sift through my list of contacts. Type out an email detailing Beverly's departure from the company. Send it to every person she may have spoken with during her time with Callahan Industries. Inform them she is no longer a point of contact or privy to company information.

By lunchtime, it feels weeks later. But the moment a soft knock sounds on my office door, the stress of the day fades to the background.

Reese.

"Come in," I say as I straighten the scattered papers on my desk and close my laptop.

The door swings open and in walks Reese, a brown bag in his hand and my favorite smile on his lips. In black slacks and a lavender button-down with the top button undone, he is sharp and delectable. *And mine.*

He closes the door, crosses the room, and sets the bag on the corner of the desk. Stepping around the desk, he swivels my chair until I face him, plants his hands on the arms, and drops his mouth to mine.

The kiss is gentle, a light caress, but powerful in its own right. A breath before I part my lips to deepen the kiss, he inches back and winks.

"No office shenanigans, boss man. Don't want to get in trouble before I officially work here."

I push out my bottom lip and give my best *hmm* whimper. "Suppose you're right." Straightening in my chair, I point to the bag. "What's on the menu?"

Reese walks around the desk, snaps up the bag, and heads for the small table and chairs in my office. He removes boxes from the bag, followed by drinks and cutlery. "Bowls from the new Greek restaurant around the corner."

Shoving away from my desk, I rise and meet him at the table, taking the seat next to him. "Hope the hype is real because I'm starving."

All conversation ceases as we dig into our lunch. Garlic and lemon and a hint of fish perfume the air. Sharp and subtle flavors dance on my tongue with each bite. And I don't know which of us moans the loudest as we eat, but I have a mind to laugh and shush Reese at the same time.

"Are you nervous?" I ask before the next bite.

He chews the rest of his bite of chicken souvlaki, takes a sip of water, and pats his lips dry with a napkin. "Yes, and no." Setting the napkin in his lap, he sets his hands on the table, palms down. "You wouldn't put me in a position to fail"—his eyes meet mine—"but I have no clue what I'm doing. And you're putting a lot of faith in me." His eyes fall to the table and study the grain with too much care.

I rest a hand over his. Caress his tanned skin with my thumb. "I would never ask you to do something I didn't think you were capable of." I duck my head until our eyes connect. "And this... not only can you do it, but you'll blow me away in the process." Bringing a hand to his chin, I tip his head back until our gazes are level. *Equals.* "The best part... I'll be by your side the entire time. I get to watch the man I love become my co-mogul."

A snort-laugh shakes his frame as the corners of his eyes crinkle and tip up. "Co-mogul, huh?"

"Damn straight." I lean in and press a chaste kiss to his lips. Lighten the moment as realization slowly creases his forehead. As Reese puts two and two together. As the gravity of his role sinks in. It's a lot to take in, but I have every confidence in him. "Reese, I believe in you. More than anyone else. And it is an honor to have you by my side."

His tawny-brown eyes glaze over as they bounce between my greens. I lift a hand and cup his cheek. Stroke the thin layer of stubble lining his jaw. Study his features as he processes what I've told him. The subtle twitch of his brows and slow blinks of his eyes. The bob of his Adam's apple before his tongue darts out to wet his lips. But those small nuances are insignificant when compared to the stiffness of his shoulders. As if what I've said is unbelievable. As if my faith in him is incomprehensible.

But I do believe in him. I do have faith in him and what we will accomplish together.

Reese has given me something no other man has. True, endless affection. A reason to wake up each morning, to breathe. Because of him, I am confident of my worth. Because of him, I am more than my career. And because of him, I have love. His love.

He has shown me what it means to *live*, what it means to *love*, and I will never take him or us for granted.

ELEVEN

REESE

Squirming in the passenger seat, all I want is to strip off my clothes, crack open a beer, and think of anything other than work.

Days into my new gig at Callahan Industries and I am ready to crawl out of my skin. It isn't Trent or the actual job—I love both. What has me constantly fidgeting is the clothes and how claustrophobic they make me feel. The starched stiffness of my shirt as it chafes my neck and throat. The annoying loose thread in my slacks that tickles the inside of my thigh every time I move, yet I can't seem to find it when I tug my pants down. The tightness of my dress shoes and cramping of my toes as the day progresses.

I've kept my aversion to the dress code to myself, not wanting to come across as bitchy or ungrateful. That and, if I complain, he will call his tailor and surrender my measurements. Within a week, I'd have new suits, dress shirts, and shoes in the closet next to his.

Like all occupations, this job has pros and cons.

Initially, I worried seeing Trent all day, every day, would not bode well for our relationship. We would grow sick of the sight of each other and the lack of alone time. I'd love the deep timbre of his voice less as he barked orders or whispered in my ear. I'd regret taking the job after moving in together and having no division of personal and business schedules. And our sex life would plummet.

But those concerns vanished by the end of day two.

The day Beverly was fired, I received keys, a photo badge, passwords, and a long, detailed description of what my job entailed. Human resources went through formalities to cover their ass, but they know who I am. Not just my name, but who I am tied to—who I belong to—as do the rest of the staff.

When I walk through the door, the staff throw smiles in my direction. Lift a hand and greet me immediately.

"Hello, Mr. Triggs."

"Good day, Mr. Triggs."

I don't have their names memorized—yet—but they sure as hell know my name. Weird as it is, their immediate respect is a shot of adrenaline in my veins. It makes me feel taller, mightier. Has me squaring my shoulders and straightening my spine. Each greeting puts a smile on my face and boosts my day.

In most large corporations, my relationship with the boss would nix my chances for the position. Fraternization would be screamed to anyone who'd listen. People who've busted their asses for years might bitch I had an unfair advantage. I'd agonize over curled lips and whispered gossip as I walked to my office.

Those concerns melted away on day one.

There has only been one drawback to the job. The damn clothes.

Every job before this, I wore loose attire. My days at the restaurant consisted of T-shirts and jeans with an apron tied low around my waist and broken-in sneakers on my feet. At the rec center, I rocked red board shorts and a whistle around my neck, my flip-flops at the base of the umbrella-shaded lifeguard stand. The low-key ensemble at both jobs fit my laid-back personality. Made my job feel less like work.

My new work wardrobe is the polar opposite.

Shirt buttoned to the base of my throat and snug on my Adam's apple. A tie beneath the collar that I reach up and adjust no less than twenty times a day. Slacks that pinch my waist, squeeze my ass and hug my thighs. The fact I haven't ripped the crotch seam yet is a damn miracle. The dress socks... I like them. I bought several pairs with fun quotes and images. Too bad the socks don't stop the shoes from rubbing blisters on my pinkie toes and heels.

"Your silence has me worried," Trent says from the driver's seat.

I blink out of my inner ramblings and twist in the seat to see him better. His hand on my thigh tightens and I lay a hand over his, tracing the length of his finger with my thumb.

"Do I need to wear ties at the office?"

After a quick glance in my direction, his eyes return to the road. He tucks his lips between his teeth, biting back a smile and possibly laughter. Then he shrugs. "Don't think it's an actual requirement for the job." A chuckle leaves his lips. "Do you not want to wear ties?" he asks, his tone playful.

I take his teasing tone and go with it. "In the bedroom? Sure. Anywhere else? Not so much."

A smirk highlights his profile. "Noted." He lifts my hand to his lips and kisses the back before setting it back on my thigh. "Any other requests?"

Not sure if this is a test or if he genuinely wants to know. Either way, I don't care. Trent won't be bothered by my not wanting to wear constrictive clothes. Hell, maybe voicing my opinion will open up new doors.

"The dressy clothes make me itchy. Figuratively and, on occasion, literally." I stare out the windshield and look at the sea of brake lights along the causeway. The mad rush of people heading home from one side of the bay to the other. As the sun sinks closer to the water and paints the sky pink and orange, I take a deep breath. "It's an adjustment and I'm trying."

"The job comes with a certain appearance."

"Yeah," I say on an exhale.

His hand squeezes my thigh. "That said, what would you rather wear? Needs to model the professionalism we uphold at CII, but I'm willing to be flexible."

His willingness to bend the rules speaks volumes and reiterates how much this man loves me. In the past year, I have learned a lot about Trent and his business. The one thing I know with certainty… he doesn't fuck around, and he holds every employee to a strict standard. No exceptions.

Until now.

My cheeks sting as a smile dons my expression. "I'll think on it this weekend."

"Good." His hand trails up my thigh, stopping just before the bulge beneath my zipper. "Speaking of the weekend, we should celebrate."

"Yeah?"

"Definitely." His fingers skirt the thickening bulge in my pants. "We haven't been to the club in months."

With Trent's busy schedule, Peyton moving out, me moving into Trent's house, and just general life responsibilities, we haven't spent much time out. A night at the club sounds like the perfect way to celebrate. The two of us, in our element. Drinks and dancing and groping for hours. And if the night ends like our previous club nights, we will be sweating for a different reason before we crash.

"A night at the club sounds perfect."

TWELVE

TRENT

The thump, thump, thump of bass vibrates my bones as we walk into Scandalous. Streams of colorful lights glow on damp skin. Earthy hops and the sweet smell of cocktails mix with sweat and sin. Lips are on lips and skin while hands tug hips closer and grind. People line the bar, crowd the tables, and flood the dance floor. Some sip fruity drinks and catch up. Others skip the drinks and search for someone to leave with later.

Electricity buzzes through the air and has the hairs on the back of my neck standing up on end.

My fingers lace with Reese's as we weave through the throng of people. I look over my shoulder and take in his bright, toothy smile as it glows under the blacklights. Returning the gesture with a smile of my own.

This right here... I have missed this part of us. Though the nightlife scene isn't an essential part of who we are, it is the root of us. Where we met. How we came together. It doesn't define us, but it is a crucial component. A piece we shouldn't ignore or forget.

Leaning into Reese, my lips ghost the shell of his ear. "God, it feels good to be here."

His fingers unthread from mine before he reaches for my shirt at my hip and tugs me closer. "Yeah, it does." His tongue darts out and swipes his bottom lip. "Should come more often."

The tips of my fingers trail up his cotton-covered chest until my palm rests over his heart. Fingers curling into a fist, I drag him forward and crush my lips to his. Shove my tongue in his mouth and taste him openly without shame.

He clutches my hips. Bruises my flesh through the denim of my jeans. Hooks his fingers in the belt loops. Keeps my hips pinned to his as our tongues taste and tangle and devour. Reese gives as good as he gets without hesitation. And in this dimly lit club, where we feel more ourselves out in the open, we let go. Give over to our primal nature. In here, we don't worry about who will see. Don't worry about what they will think or say or do.

In this place, we are *us*. Trent and Reese. Two people in love.

I break the kiss and drop my forehead to his. Work to steady my breathing. "Fuck, I love you."

He draws me back in and kisses me chastely. "Will never tire of hearing those words." Another kiss. "Love you too."

"Drink then dance?"

He nods, takes my hand, and winds us through the crowd toward the bar.

We stumble through the front door, mouths glued together. Blindly, I reach for the alarm panel, set it to home arm mode, and guide us up the stairs to the bedroom. My fingers tug at the bottom hem of Reese's shirt and yank up. The kiss breaks long enough to tear his shirt away and toss it aside.

At the second-floor landing, Reese jerks my shirt from my jeans and shoves the cotton up my chest. In one swift move, the shirt is off and flying across the room. His hands trail down the planes of my chest, the pads of his fingers grazing the ripples of my abdomen. I part my lips and suck in a stuttered breath.

"What do you want, T?"

I discerned, after our second night together, Reese loves to be dominated in the bedroom. The first time I told him to get on his knees and pull my cock out, his eyes darkened. When I told him how I wanted my cock sucked, how I wanted him to choke on my thick length, he licked his lips and did exactly as instructed. And the first time I said *good boy*... power surged in my veins as he swelled with pride. Fuck, the exchange was heady. Addictive. Insatiable.

I clamp his jaw with my fingers, tip his head slightly to the side, and ghost my lips over his chin. Breathe him in for one, two, three beats before my tongue darts out. Taste his skin. Feel the burn of his stubble against my tongue as I lick up and over his lips to the top of his philtrum.

A raspy growl consumes the air. Vibrating his chest and mine before I shove him away and walk backward.

"Hands and knees."

His eyes light up.

"Be a good boy and crawl." I point to the floor at my feet.

Without hesitation, his knees hit the carpet. Tawny eyes on my greens, his palms smack the floor next. My eyes drag over the curves of his bare spine, swallowing when I hit the dip at his lower back. The dimples above the waistband of his jeans. The proud protrusion of his ass in the air.

Eyes trained on mine, he inches across the room until he reaches my feet. Silent, he holds my gaze as he waits for the next directive. His fingers claw at the floor. Tongue darting out to moisten his eager lips. Rib cage expanding and contracting with every labored breath he takes.

My cock swells painfully seeing him like this—eager, wanton, starved—for me. The power exchange between us… nothing compares to the high it delivers. Reese at my feet, willing to do what I demand without argument, is intoxicating. Exhilarating. Liberating. The ability to be myself with him, to temporarily relinquish my rigid CEO persona, is freeing and euphoric.

Hooded eyes on his, I cup his jaw and drag my thumb over his stubbled cheek. The perfect blend of smooth and abrasive. The perfect juxtaposition when his soft lips and hot mouth consume every inch of my body.

"Unfasten my pants," I command as my hand falls away.

He inches closer and rocks back to sit on his heels. Lips a breath from the fly of my jeans, his tongue darts out and sucks in his lower lip, pinning it between his teeth. Fingers trail up the backs of my calves, loop around to the front of my legs at the knees, and spread wide as they crawl up my thighs.

Foreplay is the headiest game with Reese.

He craves my authoritarian persona in private. Subliminally begs for my imperious nature. And when I yield, undeniable gratitude shimmers in his eyes. When I subjugate him in the bedroom, make him feel small when he is anything but, he rewards my body with his. Though I command him with words, Reese retains all the power. Has the ability to deny me, to say no, to walk away.

But he doesn't. He won't. He loves the trade-off as much as I do.

He flattens his palm over the bulge beneath my zipper. Wraps his fingers around my denim-covered shaft and grinds the heel of his palm along the base of my cock. Tawny irises command my attention and demand I don't move. My jaw slackens as he strokes my length. My breaths quicken as he increases the pressure, as he teases my tip through the denim. His touch has me throbbing, aching, desperate.

My fingers comb through his locks and curl into a fist. "Take. Them. Off," I demand with a growl. "Now."

The corner of his mouth kicks up in a smirk. "Yes, *sir*."

I tip my head back. *"Fuck,"* I heave out.

Since I suggested Reese work with me at Callahan Industries, he has taken it upon himself to call me sir. At first, he'd said it in passing with a cheeky smile on his face. I'd rolled my eyes each time the word left his lips.

Until he said it in the bedroom.

And fuck, hearing the single word leave his lips before he took me in his hand, his mouth, his body…

Fire and electricity simmer beneath my skin. Heating me top to toe. Amplifying every touch he delivers as he unfastens the button and drags the zipper down the teeth of my jeans. As he peels the material down my thighs, followed by my briefs, I grip his chin and tip his head back. Swallow at the inferno burning behind his dark-honey irises.

My jeans and briefs hit the floor with a soft thump. Eyes locked on Reese, I step out and kick them aside. Lift a hand to his hair and toy with his curls. Trace my knuckle from his temple to his chin. Take his chin between my thumb and forefinger, stroking his stubble-lined jaw over and over. In my periphery, his chest expands and contracts faster. His lips part. Eyes drunk on lust and need. I drag the pad of my thumb over the soft cushion of his lips.

"Be a good boy and put my cock in your mouth," I order, desire dripping off every word.

His hooded eyes darken as his fingers wrap around my length. With slow strokes, his grip on me tightens as he moves up and down my shaft. His tongue darts out, licks his top lip, followed by his bottom. Hot and wet, he drags his tongue up the underside of my cock from root to tip. He hums in appreciation then wraps his lips around my tip and takes me to the back of his throat.

"Oh, fuck," I whisper-growl. I fist the curls at his crown and keep his rhythm steady. "Such a good fucking boy."

He moans the moment the words leave my lips, the vibration reverberating in my balls. One hand moves up and down my shaft with his mouth. The other hand finds my balls and massages. With each stroke and fondle, he edges me closer to orgasm. Skirts me closer to a high only he provides.

And then he changes pace. Slows down. Drops his hands seconds before my cock pops free from his mouth.

By the time my brain registers the shift, Reese is kissing his way up my body. Lips and tongue and teeth grazing my lower abdomen, my belly, my pecs. His short nails dragging up the sides of my torso, digging into my flesh and making their mark as he rises from the floor.

He clutches the back of my neck and crushes my lips with his. Tasting. Taking. Devouring. A moan spills from my lips and he swallows it down. Deepens the kiss and backs me up until I hit the mattress. He breaks the kiss and shoves me down on the bed. I fist my cock as his eyes coast up the length of my body. Cock a brow as his gaze lingers on my erection for one, two, three strokes before lifting to my line of sight.

"See something you want?"

"Mmm."

I jerk my chin at him. "Strip." On the next stroke up, I pinch the tip of my cock. "Then, be a good fucking boy and get on this bed." Another slow stroke. "And fuck me."

The corner of his mouth quirks up for a split second before he brings his hands to his chest. Runs them down the bare flesh of his abdomen and undoes the button and fly. Too damn slow for his own good, Reese shoves his jeans down. Beneath the denim, he is bare and hard as steel.

I moan out my appreciation, my need, my absolute desperation for him as he fists his cock.

One knee hits the mattress, then the other. He towers over me near the foot of the bed and I tighten the grip on my cock. Tug faster as his eyes drop to my throbbing erection. Then slower when he doesn't move closer. I like to watch—him jerking off, him watching me jerk off, both—but that isn't what I want right now.

Right now, I want him to spread me wide, pin my legs to the mattress, and fuck me with urgency. Like we haven't touched each other in weeks. Haven't kissed or tasted or moaned the other's name in months.

When my hand falls away, his eyes drift up my body until they meet my gaze. Brows pinched together, he tilts his head in silent question.

I bend my legs at the knee and widen them in invitation. Hold his stare and mouth, "Fuck. Me." I curl my finger in a come-hither motion, then mouth, "Now."

The corners of his mouth curve up as a mischievous smile plumps his cheeks. A playful glint twinkles in his eyes. With a single glance, I glimpse his dirty, lascivious thoughts. Then he blanks his expression and rakes his eyes down my body. Thrill ignites my bloodstream as fire licks every inch of my skin.

His palms slap the backs of my thighs before he shoves me up the bed. My head tunnels through the pillows, stopping before I smack the headboard. I watch his every move as he crawls up the bed and stops shorter than expected. Soft hands with the occasional callous trail up the backs of my thighs and force my knees closer to the mattress. Rapt, I refuse to look away as he lowers his head.

Realization dawns and I open my mouth to protest. Tell him I don't want my cock in his mouth. Not yet. But the words never leave my lips.

His tongue darts out and licks the puckered hole of my ass. Fingers dig into my thighs as he pins me harder to the mattress. A growl vibrates his mouth on my skin as his jaw relaxes and he devours me. I moan as he swirls his tongue in dizzying circles. Blindly, I reach for his hair, tugging hard once it's in my fist. He toys and teases and drives me wild.

Jagged breaths echo in the room. Sweat slicks my skin as fire snakes down my spine. Slamming my eyes shut, I roll my hips and give myself over to him. Give him the upper hand. He circles my hole once, twice, and then drags his tongue up, painting my balls, the length of my erection, and the tip of my cock in his saliva.

Unintelligible curses slip from my lips as I yank his curls.

Fingers wrapped around my cock, he buries his face

beneath my balls. Eats my ass as if it's his last meal. Makes me moan, growl, fist the bedding as I beg for more. Hands on my thighs above my ass, he inches back and hovers, gently blowing where his mouth devoured me ruthlessly. My balls tighten and I groan.

Thwack.

His palm swats my ass, and I jolt from the contact. With gentle strokes, he soothes the spot his hand struck. Then he slaps me again. My skin heats, tingles, begs for more. Precum coats the tip of my cock and I reach down to smear it over the head.

Releasing my legs, Reese stretches toward the nightstand and opens the drawer. Then he is back between my legs, a bottle of lube in his hand. It falls to the mattress as he drops to all fours, cages me in, and crushes my lips with his. He parts my lips with his tongue and devours my taste, my moans, my love for him.

Breaking the kiss, he licks and nips the line of my jaw, the column of my throat, and the hollow between my collarbones. He drifts lower. Sucks my nipples between his lips, biting the budded peaks until a hiss leaves my lips. Drags his mouth and tongue over the ridges of my abdomen, nails digging into my sides as his teeth mar my flesh.

Reese is equal parts gentle and brutal as a lover. He stirs up the most complex emotions in my head, my heart, my soul. Each soft caress leaves fire in its wake. Every bite of his nails, of his teeth, zaps me with an explosive current. But when his lips taste me... every molecule in my makeup comes to life. Gravitates toward him. Vibrates with need. Begs for another hit.

His lips abandon my skin, and I immediately miss the feel of him. He rocks back on his heels. Grabs the bottle of lube, pops the lid, and squirts liquid in his palm. He snaps the lid closed and tosses the bottle aside. Coating the length of his erection, my eyes fall to his hand as he strokes himself. Jaw slack, lust clouding his vision as he watches me watch him.

And then he drags his lube-coated fingers over the seam of my ass. The pad of his thumb circles my tight hole, over and over. On the third circuit, he adds pressure. Slowly pushes in as I drag in a sharp breath. In and out. In and out. His thumb teases the tight hole before coming away.

Reese scoots closer and I push up on my elbows. He lines up the thick head of his cock with my ass. I stop breathing as I wait for him to thrust forward.

But he doesn't.

My eyes dart to his in question, and what I see knocks the last ounce of air from my lungs. I fall back to the mattress and lift a hand to his face. Cup his cheek for three strokes of my thumb and then let go.

Inch by painstakingly slow inch, he lowers himself until his breath paints my lips. His mouth drops to mine, and he kisses me with a slow, gentle force. Strong arms bracket my face, his fingers toying with the short strands of my hair. He sedates me with his lips and the unspoken message they speak.

He kisses a lazy trail to my ear and sucks the lobe

between his lips. "Love you so fucking much, T," he whispers, a breath before his hips rock forward and his cock fills me fully.

I band an arm around his waist and trail my free hand up his spine. My fingers dive into his curls and guide him back to my mouth. Gazes locked and lips ghosting his, I reply with equal tenderness. "Not like I love you."

And then we get lost in each other for hours.

THIRTEEN

REESE

What the hell?

The past few weeks have been a major adjustment. New jobs are always a challenge. New jobs in an unfamiliar line of work are exhausting. But every day I sit at my desk at Callahan Industries, I feel more at ease in my role. More confident with my responsibilities.

Overseeing finances sits at the top of my daily to-do list. Someone else logs the figures into spreadsheets from bank statements and invoices. My job is to review, compare, and monitor the numbers for accuracy. A tedious task, it isn't for the faint of heart. The more I stare at the figures, the more they swirl together.

But this is different. My eyes aren't buggy.

Something is off. *Way off.*

Pushing away from the desk, I rise to my feet, scoop up the laptop, and exit my office. In three strides, I knock on Trent's open door, step inside, and close the door behind me. The jovial smile on his lips falls away when he sees the concern on my face.

"What's wrong?"

Taking the seat across from him at his desk, I set the laptop down and spin it so we both have a view of the screen. I highlight a figure on the spreadsheet and shake my head.

"This number should be much higher."

We stare at the income from the San Francisco branch of Callahan Industries, a location that opened its doors last year. Through last week's report, the site had steady earnings with a slight increase each week. Reviewing the recent figures, there is a noticeable dip in revenue on the spreadsheet. Karina, a long-term, trusted employee in the finance department, populates this particular log with figures from the bank accounts. She doesn't cross-reference them with invoices and payments, that duty belongs to Tracy.

It isn't in my job description to study itemized finances, but this weird vibe had me digging deeper today.

Trent turns the laptop to face him fully and drags it closer before tilting the screen. I stand and drag a chair around the desk to sit beside him. The arm of my chair grazes the arm of his as we lean in to study the screen.

His eyes dart back and forth as he reviews and compares the numbers on the spreadsheet before toggling to the detailed list of invoices I have up on another document. With each new line he reads, his face turns a deeper shade of red.

"What the fuck?" he mutters with a growl.

His hand freezes over the keys as his eyes lose focus. Anger charges the air in the room. Trent stiffens, his shoulders and spine rigid. A feral look flashes in his eyes as he stares at the screen. At the audible grind of his molars, Trent is a force to be reckoned with.

I lay a hand on his forearm and he startles in place. "Tell me what to do, T."

His breathing spikes, his unbridled rage evident in each exhale. I keep my hand on his forearm. Let it be an anchor to ground him as he cools off. One by one, his breaths grow quieter, less intense. He twists in his chair and looks me square in the eyes.

Anger dilates his pupils, setting his lips in a firm, flat line, flaring his nostrils. He isn't angry with me. Trent is angry at the situation, at whoever is responsible.

"Dig," he says in a stern tone. "As deep as you can. And don't say a word to anyone." His eyes narrow for a split second. "*No one.*"

To anyone else, his harsh words would be taken as a personal jab, a slap in the face. But I don't take them as such. His words, his tone, his fury, are aimed at the thief. The person that fucked with his empire. The person he trusted and who broke their loyalty. The person that stole from him.

And now, with the exception of me, his trust in others is gone. Until we get answers, he trusts no one outside this room. Not without time, discovery, and a shitload of vetting.

I nod and stand, moving the chair back to the other side of the desk. Closing the lid on the laptop, I swipe it up from the desk and head for the door. If I thought Trent had worked endless hours before, both of us were in for a surprise. Until this is resolved, our jobs will be our life.

"Reese." My name on his lips stops me at the door.

I spin to face him. "Yeah?"

"Thank you."

The corner of my mouth lifts in a sympathetic half smile. "No need to thank me, T. Just glad I found it now and not down the road."

He tips his head to the side and his neck cracks. "Me too." He takes a deep breath. "This is top priority until it's sorted out. The other shit on your agenda, we'll get through them together at the end of each day."

"Understood."

I twist the handle and open the door. As I step through, he calls my name again.

"Love you, Triggs."

I wink at him. "Love you, Callahan."

I take a deep breath as I step into the hall. *This is bad.* Had I not found it, it could have been a hell of a lot worse.

Jesus fucking Christ.

The deeper I dig, the longer this rabbit hole goes.

Elbows on the table, I drop my head in my hands and

fist my hair. Close my eyes and visualize the end of this nightmare coming sooner rather than later. Suck in a ragged breath and try to ease the stress from my stiff muscles.

In the past seventy-two hours, I have journeyed down a long and well-disguised path of deceit. Though the brunt of the losses started when Beverly Prescott took her position at Callahan Industries, it isn't solely her who is responsible. Two others have joined the mix. Two people that have worked for Trent for more than three years.

Neal from payroll has pilfered small amounts from every hourly employee's paycheck for the last year and a half. Company-wide, there are nearly five hundred hourly paid employees. From the cleaning crew to secretaries to hospitality staff and more. Each pay period, this man has stolen anywhere from one dollar—in the beginning—to fifteen dollars from every hourly paid person. He adds the deduction to their stub—the name varies from insurance costs, retirement funds, tip fees or bonus taxes, depending on the employee—to make the missing money appear legitimate. And through all the evidence I've unearthed, not many have questioned the missing funds. The few that have, Neal has issued them an additional check—money from Callahan Industries and not the pot where he has filtered the money—to reimburse the loss. Then, he stopped skimming from their checks.

Altogether, Neal has embezzled close to seventy-five thousand dollars. And I am nowhere near done looking at everything he has had his hands in.

The other person slowly building a rap sheet is Tracy

from finance. Her list of crimes isn't as steep as Neal's but has climbed steadily in the past few months.

Responsible for matching billing itemization to the bank account spreadsheets, Tracy has fudged numbers to her advantage. A minor adjustment to the deposit amounts on the spreadsheet. The addition of a few small company purchases here and there. Like Neal, Tracy has access to the company "checkbook" and credit card and has purchased items online or deposited money in her personal account under the guise of work expenses. Several online purchases were traced to the company's local Amazon account. I accessed and retrieved the order history, then stared slack-jawed at the screen as I scrolled pages of purchases. Books, purses, graphic T-shirts, mugs. The list was endless and her boundaries were nil.

To date, Tracy has stolen more than fifty thousand dollars' worth of merchandise and cash. Her trail was not as intricately masked as Neal's, which makes her crimes much easier to slap with fines and jail time.

Trent plops down in the chair next to me and sets a tumbler with two fingers of bourbon on the table. Two may not be enough when I divulge the latest news.

"Give me details."

I rock my head in my hands and tug my hair before releasing it to sit straight. Tilting my head, I meet Trent's gaze. Worry lines crease the corners of his eyes and wrinkle his brow. Light-purple half-moons paint the skin beneath his lower lashes. Over the past three days, he has aged a decade from the stress of the situation.

Lifting the tumbler to my lips, I swallow half the contents before setting the glass back down.

"Neal in payroll and Tracy in finance. Between the two of them, almost a hundred and twenty-five thousand in the last twenty months."

"*Fuck, fuck, fuck.*"

My thoughts exactly. "Not that you didn't know this, but you need an attorney. Someone that has your absolute trust. Because this"—I wave a hand toward my laptop—"is not petty theft."

Trent brings his own glass to his lips and downs every drop before slamming the tumbler on the table. His entire frame vibrates with rage. A rage incomparable to what I feel. Anger, frustration and exhaustion have been constant as I've dug for answers. But my indignation is child's play next to Trent's fury.

"You think they're in cahoots?"

I shrug and speak honestly. "Not sure. I need someone with better tech skills for that. Someone who can look at digital trails through coding. Not necessarily a hacker, but someone with an equivalent skill set." I down the last of my bourbon. "Got any computer gurus you trust implicitly?"

Dragging a hand over his face, Trent groans as he pinches the bridge of his nose. Humorless laughter spills from his lips as he drops his hand with a thud to the table. "I trusted the two fuckers stealing from me." He drags in a jagged breath and meets my gaze with uncertain eyes. "How the hell am I to know if I can trust anyone else in the company? How the hell can I ask someone to look into this from within?" Wood creaks as he grips the edge of the table. "It's probably isolated, but this puts a major fracture in my trust in anyone." He lays a hand on my thigh. "With the exception of you, of course."

"Never thought otherwise." I lace our fingers together. "Maybe we bring Radford in for a meeting. Play it off as making sure tech security is in place after what happened with Prescott. Let him do most of the talking. We analyze his answers, his body language and overall vibe." I shrug. "Then, we go from there." I give his fingers a squeeze. "If we need to hire someone outside the company, then that's what we do. But we shouldn't wait much longer, and we need to be discreet. They can't know we suspect anything. Shit will tank quickly if they suspect we're onto them."

He runs a hand through his hair. Grips the back of his neck and sighs heavily. "This is beyond fucked up."

"Agreed."

"After all the bullshit my father dealt with in business, I swore I'd never be in his shoes. I vetted people with a fine-tooth comb. Dug up every ding on their record and made decisions based on evidence." Wood scrapes wood as Trent pushes back on his chair and rises. "How did I not see this? People start shit like this early on and leave trails."

"True." I scoot away from the table, stand, and stretch my limbs. "But maybe these people worked for smaller companies before you. Maybe they got away with more because no one looked over their shoulder or checked their work. And before anyone caught on to what they'd done, they jumped ship. Found a shinier prize to target." I wince, hating that Trent and his company are the shinier prize.

"Let's take a break tonight." He wraps my hand with his and leads me to the kitchen. "Help me make dinner. Food and wine and nonwork conversation." Pleading evergreen irises hold mine. "Please."

Dinner and drinks won't make this nightmare end, but we need some semblance of normalcy. Something to steal the limelight for an hour or two. Something less stressful and more intimate. A night off.

I sidle up to Trent at the open fridge as he grabs butcher-wrapped salmon steak, carrots and broccoli before closing the door. He hands me the vegetables. "Cut these to roast with the potatoes and garlic in the basket." He points to the produce basket on the counter. "I'll ready the fish."

As I rinse the produce, he pours heavy-handed glasses of chardonnay. We move in tandem in the kitchen, and before long, our meal is plated. We park on the couch with dinner, flip on the television, and get lost in fictional cinematic bliss.

And when bedtime arrives, we ignore the dirty dishes and take the stairs two at a time. Strip each other bare at the foot of the bed and lose ourselves in one another for hours.

Our heads hit the pillow, my back to his front, our limbs tangled and eyes heavy. Soft snores float through the room as Trent's frame relaxes. I drift off to the rhythmic sound of his snores and rise and fall of his chest.

Just before sleep takes me, another thought hits... *Everything will work itself out.* Not sure how, but I feel resolution in my bones. *Everything happens for a reason.* And damn if I am not determined to find answers.

Reese sits with me at the table in my office. His fingers fly across the laptop keys as he digs further for evidence of misappropriation. This whole Neal and Tracy situation has me livid. On the cusp of inflicting violence. If not for Reese, my knuckles would be bloody and my wrists in cuffs. He has been my sounding board through this bullshit.

Enraged with each development, I endeavor to not dwell on the unchangeable. The past can't be erased. What's done is done.

Now, my attention is centered on reparations and preventing further damage.

Step one in the process… speak with Radford. Inconspicuously interrogate him and determine whether or not I trust him. If deemed trustworthy, we proceed with step two—putting our hands in the slime-infested embezzlement waters to find secrets and answers.

Please, I beg you, let it be an isolated issue.

"Should be here any minute," Reese mumbles as he adds more to the long list of crimes committed by Neal and Tracy.

Taking the handkerchief from my pocket, I wipe my brow then stow the cloth. I clench and straighten my fingers over and over. Shoving away from the table, I rise from the chair and go to the mini-fridge hidden beneath the coffee bar.

"Drink?"

Reese stops typing and peeks over his shoulder. "Coffee, please."

I place a mug under the drip, insert a pod of Reese's favorite dark roast, and press the brew button. While coffee fills the mug, I grab a bottle of orange juice and the cream from the fridge. I tear open and empty a couple packets of stevia. Add cream until the coffee swirls from black to light brown. As I set the mug in front of Reese, a knock sounds at the door.

"Come in," I call out as I take my seat. Radford steps through the door with an apprehensive smile on his face. "Close the door, please."

His smile falls, and he swallows before shutting the door. One foot in front of the other, he makes his way to the conference table. Almost undetectable, his brows twitch and eyes narrow in evident confusion.

"Everything alright, Mr. Callahan?" His eyes shift to Reese—who hasn't looked up or acknowledged Radford—then focus on me once more.

"Please, Radford, take a seat."

I study his every move as he pulls out a chair, skirts

around the seat, and finally sits. His hands drop to his lap, hidden by the wood table. He leans back and relaxes his shoulders. Appears at ease. But I don't miss the indecision and distress radiating off him.

It isn't every day your boss calls you into his office without warning, then tells you to close the door.

In my younger years, anytime I got called in to speak with the boss—whether it was my father at Callahan Financial or the manager from the small retail job I worked for two years as a teen—it was always an unsettling feeling. Like wanting to shit your pants and throw up at the same time.

"Want anything to drink?" I offer.

A squishy *V* forms between his brows a beat before he swallows. "Uh… water," he croaks out.

I grab a bottle of water from the fridge, set it in front of him, and return to my seat.

"Radford, I'd like to start this meeting off with two things. One—everything we're about to discuss needs to remain between the three of us. Not even your family hears a peep. No exceptions. Period."

He nods, twists off the bottle cap, takes a long pull of water, then secures the lid.

"Two—you aren't in trouble."

His body visibly sags in the chair.

"But"—I hold up a finger—"I am having trust issues with staff right now."

For a beat, I remain silent. Let him digest what little I've said. Study his physical response to my statement. The way he cradles the water bottle. The minor tilt of his head as he tries to decipher who or what has me on edge.

What I don't see are nervous tics. Sweat on his brow or temples. Fidgety fingers or a shaky frame from leg bounces beneath the table. Constant nose twitches or blinking eyes.

His eyes haven't left mine—except to glance at Reese—since entering the room. Still, I plan to tread lightly. Radford may not have given me reason to mistrust him, but this is a delicate situation.

Uncapping my juice, I take a sip and then set it on a coaster. I toy with the lid and watch it spin on the table for one, two, three revolutions before it falls flat on the table.

"It has come to our attention"—my eyes lift to meet his—"some employees have been deceptive in their role at Callahan Industries."

Reese stops typing on his laptop and finally looks at Radford, whose eyes have widened exponentially.

"Not sure what to say, Mr. Callahan."

"Not much you can say, Radford. But we do have a request."

"Okay."

I gesture to Reese. "Mr. Triggs."

In my periphery, I witness the slight change in Reese's posture. Hear the almost inaudible hitch in his breath. I make a mental note of his reaction and stow it away to address in the future. If we weren't here to discuss egregious news about the business, I'd ask Radford to come back in thirty minutes.

"Thank you, Mr. Callahan," Reese states, his tone

meant to be serious, but I pick up on the faint lilt. He nods infinitesimally, shifts his gaze to Radford, and dons a mask of solemnity. "Callahan Industries has suffered at the hands of thieves. I've spent the past three and a half days investigating and have hit the point where help is required."

Radford sits straighter in his chair, inches closer to the table, rests his forearms on the wood and leans in. "And you believe I may be able to help?"

Reese nods. "Exactly. Before we get into the nitty-gritty, we need to again express how crucial it is for you to keep this under wraps." Reese picks up the manilla folder on his right and sets it between us, opening the folder and removing the NDA I had Vincent, my attorney, draft this morning. "This is a nondisclosure agreement. Please read it over, but it states all matters regarding this situation are to remain one-hundred-percent confidential. Tasks can only be done on Callahan Industries–approved technology, in the office, and only during business hours. For this project, any overtime you accrue has been preapproved — within a reasonable limit, of course."

Reese slides the document across the table, then laces his fingers and rests his forearms on the table. Radford thumbs through the pages, his eyes widening as the gravity of the situation sinks in. Several minutes of silence pass as he reads each line. When he reaches the end, he straightens the pages, looks across the table, purses his lips, and nods.

"Do you have a pen?" he asks.

From my suit jacket, I pluck a pen from the inside

pocket, twist it, and offer it to Radford. He signs on the line, lays the pen on top, and pushes the document toward us. I flip to the back page and sign, then give it to Reese to do the same.

With legalities out of the way, we dive headfirst into this nightmare.

Over the next hour, we spell out our discoveries. Reese forwards the detailed log of findings to Radford's email. We outline a plan of attack and schedule regular check-ins via phone, video or in person. Since tech support isn't often needed on a regular basis, we limit in-person meetings and agree to conduct them during times with fewer staff present.

Maintaining appearances, we end the meeting and agreed to say Reese was having laptop issues, if anyone were to ask. Radford leaves my office exactly how he came, with nothing in his hands.

He opens the door and peers over his shoulder. "If you have any other issues with the laptop, Mr. Triggs, please reach out." The facade up firmly in place for prying ears.

"Appreciate the assistance," Reese replies before the door closes.

Reese spins in his chair to face me head-on. "Thoughts?"

"Antsy, as I am bringing in another person, it's necessary." My tongue darts out and wets my lips. "My eyes were on him every second. I trust my gut and our decision to work with him."

"Me too." Reese sips his now cold coffee. "My typing

while you talked didn't distract him. And the energy in the room… I got no bad vibes."

"Me either."

Reese rests a hand on my knee. "We'll get this sorted out. Promise." He gives my knee a gentle squeeze. "Until then, we keep a vigilant eye on things. Don't say anything we wouldn't normally. More importantly, we go about business as usual."

Playing ignorant with staff irritates me almost as much as the problem. But Reese is right. To catch the thieves, we let them believe everyone is clueless about their crimes.

"Well, don't forget business as usual also includes our trip next week."

When Reese and I started dating, work trips lost their excitement. Before our relationship, trips were adventurous. Business consumed the majority of my time but exploring the city was never not an option. I love Tampa, love the bustling life of big cities, but no two are identical. Bumper-to-bumper traffic is the same everywhere, but the attitude of commuters changes the drive. Skyscrapers shine differently in the sun when surrounded by water or trees or mountains. The biggest surprise is how unique life is in each place. While some make you claustrophobic, others make you feel at home.

And I look forward to time with Reese outside of our small city bubble.

My favorite smile brightens Reese's expression. "Can't wait to see the world with you, sir."

He rises from his chair, plants his hands on my

armrests, and drops his lips to mine. The kiss is soft, sweet and ends way too soon.

"Mmm. Something about the taste of coffee on your lips does things to me."

Swiping up his laptop from the table, he starts for the door. "Consider it foreplay." He winks. "Meet for lunch?"

"Absolutely. I'll have Dale order food. One o'clock?"

"Perfect, *sir*." He cocks a brow then disappears out the door.

Prior to suggesting Reese work for Callahan Industries, I questioned mixing personal and business. My father said mingling the two was the perfect equation for failure. Only one would survive. Until Reese, I agreed with him.

Then life changes. Your view of people sharpens. Your perception of what matter shifts. The world evolves, as does business, and you must choose whether or not to move forward or remain stagnant.

Would it be bad for business if Reese and I split? God, yes. My devastation would bleed into my workload. Would render me defunct. Broken. Which is why I tread lightly with the offer.

Reese and I have been in a committed relationship for more than a year. Though I *broke up* with him before every trip, neither of us was unfaithful. I'd thought my frequent trips would strain our relationship—on occasion, it did—but we never let go. Considering we'd never put down roots before our relationship, our commitment to each other speaks volumes.

Hiring my boyfriend to be my second-in-command was risky. But damn, it was the best decision I've made.

Reese isn't some random guy. He isn't a fling. Dare I think it, let alone say it aloud… Reese Triggs is my match. The man that settles the crazy in my hectic life. The man that makes the world more stable under my feet.

He is the best decision I made. Saying yes. Keeping him. Loving him.

Without Reese, I am a man without direction. Without him, I am a shell of myself.

"Damn, did I luck out," I mutter to myself.

And with each breath I take, I will prove myself worthy of Reese's heart.

FIFTEEN

REESE

SALTY AIR FILLS MY LUNGS AS A LIGHT BREEZE FROM San Francisco Bay sweeps hair across my cheek. The early fall sun warms my face while the crisp, cool air has me tugging at my long sleeves. I drag in a deep breath, count to three, and sigh on the exhale. My stomach growls as the breeze wafts scents from local restaurants and cafés. Fresh baked bread and cheese from the pizzeria, the nutti-ness of brewed coffee from the café, and the sweet pungency of smoked salmon.

At the end of Pier 39, my eyes scan the bay.

To the left, the iconic Golden Gate Bridge begs to be seen with its rusty-red paint, high towers, and lengthy suspension cables. Trent promises we will cross the bridge and get a better view of it and the city from a less popu-lous lookout point before we leave. Either way, it steals my breath to see it in person.

Straight ahead, the island of Alcatraz stares back with

ominous eyes and cursed walls. Another tourist adventure on our to-do list while here. Thrill hums through my veins at the idea of walking the corridors and seeing where legendary criminals spent their final years. It is said the island is haunted… if you believe such things.

And off to the right is the San Francisco-Oakland Bay Bridge. Though it doesn't bear bright colors like the Golden Gate, the bridge is massive and begs to be seen.

Trent tightens his hold around my waist as he rests his chin on my shoulder. His body molds to mine as a soft sigh leaves his lips. My fingers weave with his before I turn my head to kiss him.

Though we don't hide our relationship publicly back home, being this intimate out in the open doesn't happen often in Florida. We live in an area where the majority accept same-sex couples. It isn't often we get prolonged stares or curled lips, but it happens.

Here, in the heart of San Francisco, I have never felt more comfortable in my own skin and sharing intimacy with my boyfriend in public.

This city is… liberating.

"Hungry?" Trent asks when he breaks the kiss.

"Starved." In more ways than one.

He takes a step back, reaches for my hand, and laces our fingers together before guiding us through the throng of people. The walkway between the shops isn't so crowded we can't walk side by side, but residents and tourists alike pack the promenade.

Trent steers us toward the Italian seafood restaurant

on the pier, and soon, we are seated at a cloth-covered table with a view of the water. As my eyes roam the tables, my frame relaxes into the chair. With the white linens, goblet water glasses, and folded cloth napkins between more forks and spoons than I typically use in one meal, the restaurant gives the appearance of fine dining. But the more my eyes wander, the more this place boasts the aura of casual. Most people wear jeans and T-shirts with sneakers rather than button-downs, slacks, and dresses.

Compared to the few pricier places Trent has taken me back home, this place feels more us. Elegant, yet relaxed. Less stuffy and more *we welcome everyone*.

We order a bottle of pinot noir, an appetizer to share, and our meals before the server gathers our menus and heads for the server alley between the kitchen and dining room.

My eyes drift out the window and across the water, watching the boats as they move through various parts of the bay. This city is nothing short of busy, but it is a different kind of busy from home. Everything here feels alive and fresh and receptive. Vivacious energy lives in the air. Begs for you to feel it, absorb it, experience it.

I love home. But I can't deny loving here too.

My lips curve up as Trent's fingers cascade lightly over the top of my hand. Eyes shifting from the window to him, my breath catches in my throat. My heart jumps a gear and pound, pound, pounds in the confines of my rib cage. Trent could be in tattered clothes and in desperate need of a shower and he would still be beautiful. But right now, in this place where we can be ourselves so freely, this laid-back look, this dreamy, lovestruck look, renders me speechless, breathless, jittery.

"Love you, Reese," he says just over the background noise of the dining room. He weaves our fingers, his thumb stroking the base of mine as his green eyes soften. "More than I thought possible."

This garners the biggest, dopiest smile from my lips.

I never intended to fall in love with this man, but fall I did. Hard and fast. Without effort. Without question. Without a chance of survival if he chose to leave one day.

But as I hold the dark-green depths of his eyes in this very moment, I know every single day of my future will include him—us.

"Love you too, Trent." I lift his hand to my lips and kiss his knuckles in turn. "So much it makes me breathless."

The server sidles up to the table seconds after my proclamation. After showing us the bottle, she pops the cork, fills two glasses halfway, then sets the bottle to the side and walks off. The remainder of dinner goes by in a blur of mouthwatering dishes, more wine, and endless smiles and laughter.

I love this city, and by the end of dinner, it is blatantly obvious Trent loves it here too.

After dinner, we indulge in the best tiramisu to hit my taste buds. The moans this single piece of dessert elicits should be criminal. Once I've made a fool of myself over the chocolate espresso sweet course, Trent settles the check.

With his hand on my lower back, my skin heating from the small public display of ownership, Trent guides us out of the restaurant. His hand doesn't leave its spot, his fingers painting soft strokes as we move through the thinning crowd. The warmth from his touch intensifies with each brush of his fingers. My breath stutters as his fingers leisurely purposely inch up the fabric of my shirt. Graze the bare flesh beneath.

"Coffee?"

I suck in a breath and turn to look at him, the spot between my brows tight. "Huh?"

The corners of his mouth curve up in a suggestive, cocky smile. "Before we head back to the hotel, do you want a coffee?"

Caffeine probably isn't the best idea this late in the evening. Then again, my body is all out of whack from the three-hour time difference, so it won't hurt. Plus, with the way Trent is touching me, teasing me, waking every live wire in my body, I don't see us sleeping anytime soon.

"Coffee sounds perfect."

Trent orders a *normal* coffee—café Americano—while I opt for the Biscoff latte. If the caffeine doesn't keep me up, surely it will be the sugar from this and dessert.

We sip our drinks as we stroll the waterfront hand in hand. Rose and lavender and sherbet-orange paint the darkening blue sky; the Golden Gate Bridge and mountains a spectacular addition to the sunset I'd never see back home. Several pedestrians pause on the sidewalk to snap pictures of the skyline. When we reach a less crowded spot, I jerk to a stop.

"What is it?" Trent asks, ridges marring his brow.

I drop his hand and fish my phone from my pocket. "Tourist time," I answer, holding up my phone and wiggling it.

Near the edge of the sidewalk, where it meets the sand, I open the camera on my phone and flip it to selfie mode. Trent takes my drink and his and sets them down. He bands his arm around my waist and tugs me close. The action makes me smile instantly, and I take the first photo. My finger taps the button, again and again, capturing our smiles, our laughter, my lips on his, and more.

At some point, I stop taking pictures and shove my phone in my pocket. His hands land on my hips and mine clutch his cheeks. Without a care in the world, we kiss in the biggest public display.

In this city, we are just two people in love. In this city, no one shames us for who we are.

At the end of the week, we have to leave. Part of me wants to stay, though. Part of me says this is where I belong. Where we belong.

Chest heaving, Trent breaks the kiss and drops his forehead to mine. "Let's go."

With a subtle nod, I lean back and lace my fingers with his. He fetches my drink and hands it over before picking up his own. Then, he all but drags me a few blocks to the hotel.

The moment we step into the suite, our drinks are forgotten.

We strip each other bare as we stumble toward the bedroom. With lips and tongues and teeth, we worship and devour and love one another. I moan his name as he plunges into my ass. Fist the sheets with my face pressed into the mattress. And before he comes inside me, before I paint the sheet with cum, he pulls out and flips me on my back. Pushes himself inside me once more. Drops his weight over me, into me, and strokes ever so slowly as he drops his lips to mine.

He kisses me drunk. Makes love to my mouth, my body, and my heart with each measured stroke of his tongue and cock. Strong forearms bracket my head while I reach up to frame his face with my hands. His fingers toy with the length of my hair as he deepens the kiss. As he consumes me. Marks my soul as only his to touch, forever.

And it is with that thought, I orgasm. Paint our chests with my undiluted love for him, for us, for everything we will be.

"Oh, fuck, Reese." He crushes my lips with his. Rocks his hips faster. Plunges into me harder. Curls his fingers in my hair and tugs until fire stings my scalp. "Fuck, I love you."

And before I respond in kind, the heat of his orgasm floods my body. Has me clutching his ass and holding him in place. He drops his mouth to where my shoulder and neck meet, his teeth clamping down as the last of him spills into me.

He collapses on my chest, lungs heaving as he kisses the skin along my collarbone. My legs circle his hips, hook at the ankles and pin him in place. And for a beat, we lie there.

My fingers comb through his hair with the barest of touch. "I love you, T."

Pushing up onto his elbows, his green irises glow as they look down. "Love you more."

SIXTEEN

TRENT

My gut twists for the umpteenth time this morning and I press a loose fist to my stomach. I have no idea what kicked this into motion, but something is… *wrong.*

"Not hungry?" Reese asks, eyeing my barely touched breakfast as he finishes his.

The tines of my fork push the scrambled eggs around the plate. I should eat more, it angers me to waste food, but every time I load the fork and consider taking a bite, my stomach cramps.

Did the seafood from dinner not sit well with me? Can't be that. I would have felt the effects shortly after. Maybe I drank too much wine. A drink with dinner or after a rough day is normal, but mixed with the trip and work chaos, it might have been too much last night.

My stomach wrings again, and I mentally admonish the organ. *Stop it.*

Blaming this feeling on bad food or too much alcohol

doesn't fit. No, this… this is something else. Something just out of reach. Something instinctual waving its hand and begging for attention. But what?

Reese and I are good. More than good. Since we landed in San Francisco, our relationship has only gotten stronger, better, more intense. This trip, this place, has brought us closer together. Connected us on a new level.

The twinge in my gut does a nauseating flip and I slap a hand over my mouth. Beneath my palm, my skin feels cool, clammy. "Something isn't right," I mutter through my hand.

Reese's fork clangs on his plate. He pushes back on his chair and is at my side in two strides.

"Are you going to be sick? Do you need help to the bathroom?"

I shake my head but wonder if throwing up will help whatever is causing the problem. "I don't think so." My words a borderline question. Closing my eyes, I take a breath and think of anything other than the cramp in my midsection. As the room comes back into view, I feel incrementally better. Picking up a slice of toast, I take a small bite and say, "Maybe some water. Please."

Reese darts from the two-seater table, enters the suite's small kitchen and fetches a bottle of water from the fridge. He returns to my side seconds later, twisting off the cap and shoving the bottle in my hand.

I swallow down one sip, then another. Little by little, my stomach relaxes. Recapping the bottle, I sigh. "Thank you. Not sure what happened, but it appears to have settled."

"Should we cancel the meeting?"

I focus on my body for a minute. Do a mental scan head to toe. Stretch my limbs, my fingers, and toes. Feel the expansion and contraction of my chest with each inhalation. Implore my stomach to remain calm.

"No," I say with a shake of my head. "I'm better." Reese narrows his eyes. "Swear," I vow.

His tawny eyes soften before he rests a hand on my shoulder. "Fine." His fingers give a gentle squeeze. "But if you start feeling sick again, the meeting is done. Period."

I smirk. "Yes, sir."

After I finish the last of my toast, we tidy up our dishes. Reese slips on a sharp gray button-down and I watch, mesmerized, as he fastens each button. I button my own shirt and slip a tie around my neck. Loop it into a knot and slide it to the base of my throat. Reese licks his lips in appreciation and I cock a brow in return. I don my suit jacket while Reese drapes a blazer over his arm.

A few steps in his direction, I press my lips to his. Give him a kiss that ends far too soon.

And then my hand is on his lower back as I guide us out of the room.

Dazed, I blink a few times. "Sorry, Catarina. What?"

Across the table, Catarina winces and shrinks in her chair. "I, uh…" Her eyes dart to Reese, then hesitantly return to my gaze. "I updated your assistant," she says in a staccato. "She said there'd been a breach, and she needed the account log-on information for our location. She said she'd reset it and provide the new details soon."

My elbows thump on the conference room table. I drop my head in my hands and smash the heels of my palms to my closed eyes. Curl my fingers in my hair and growl out my frustration.

One vertebra at a time, I straighten my spine and drop my hands to the table. Inhale deeply to cool the fire dancing in my veins. Do my damnedest to not scream at one of my most valuable employees. "Did you not think to call anyone and verify her before giving out confidential information?" My fingers curl and flex. "An email went out weeks ago that a woman working closely with me was terminated." I grind my molars and take another deep breath. "Did you not read the email?"

She twiddles a pen between her fingers. "Patrick has been reading and relaying my emails." Her fingers drop the pen when she sees me eyeing her nervous tell. "He said a woman was let go, but didn't say who she was or what level of authority she'd had." Her eyes fall shut as she pinches the bridge of her nose. "*Shit*," she mutters. "Shit, shit, shit." She opens her eyes and meets my stony gaze. "I'll understand if you fire me. I am one hundred percent at fault. I was just trying to delegate—"

I hold up my hand to stop her. "Catarina, you aren't fired."

Her entire frame sighs.

"But there will be severe consequences. Something we'll discuss another time. For now, we need to put out this fire." I twist in my seat to face Reese. "Call Radford and update him. Then call Dale and do the same. He'll know who to relay news to." Before leaving Tampa, I opened up to Dale about the office mishaps. Gave him the basics and asked him to keep an eye out for suspicious activity while Reese and I were out of town. I needed someone else in our corner. Someone who'd report to me, Reese, Radford, and Beth Anne if anything popped up.

"On it," Reese says as he rises from his chair and steps away from the table.

Once Reese is out of earshot, I sit in silence, my gaze laser focused on Catarina.

It took years for me to understand, but my father always said silence is the best way to learn the most from a person. *"Remain silent and let their body language and lips do all the talking."* And every single time, it works. Big or small, all details come to light as I sit in wait.

Brows pulled tight at the middle, teeth nibbling on the corner of her bottom lip, Catarina's gaze refuses to look anywhere but at me. The tip of her finger taps the table at a pace too fast to count. Her lips part to speak, but she snaps them shut. Then she repeats the action. Twice.

Catarina and I have always shared a comfortable business relationship. As I conducted interviews for upper management for the San Francisco location, she had been the one person I felt the most right about. She is personable, innovative, perceptive, and sharp as hell—in business and life. When she walks in a room, heads turn and conversations quiet. It isn't her beauty that commands attention—though, she is stunning. It is her presence, her aura, her energy that screams for you to take notice.

She is a force to be reckoned with and won't go down without a fight.

Except now.

Today is the first time I have seen her appear so defeated. Spine curled and shoulders caved forward. Fidgeting worse than a child lying to a parent. Red rims her glassy eyes. A slight wobble to her chin.

She doesn't need to say she is sorry. I hear her apology in every unspoken word. See it in the slump of her spine and in the threat of her tears.

"Trent, I—"

I hold up my hand again. "Some people need to hear the words, need apologies verbalized." Leaning forward, I reach across the table and rest my hand over hers to settle the nervous tap of her fingers. I give her what I hope is a soft smile. "Without saying it, I know you're upset and remorseful." Pulling back, I recline into my chair. "Not going to lie. This is a mess. A big fucking mess." I purse my lips. "But it will get fixed. And the people responsible will be handled."

Her face pales. "What about me? What about Patrick?"

"When I have a day or two to mull this over, I'll write up the formal disciplinary action. Some permissions will be temporarily withheld. Controls you once headed will be monitored for a period. Salary increases and bonuses will be on pause until said period ends. As for Patrick, his penalties will be less severe. But you delegated duties, and he didn't properly relay critical information. That isn't just on you, but him too."

At the fallen look on her face, I sigh.

"Cat, you are one of the few people I hold in high esteem within the company. But I can't play favorites right now. Had this been anyone else, depending on the severity of the situation, I'd have done the same or worse."

"You're right." She nods. "I just hate that I put the company in jeopardy in the first place."

"Actually"—I hold up a finger—"it was me who did that. I hired the woman responsible and gave her too much access too soon." My hands drag up my face and into my hair. "Was trying to lighten my load. Not work as much. Be there for Reese. Have a life."

Her brows shoot up as she points toward the door. "Reese? The guy with you?"

Often, I forget not everyone is aware of my relationship with Reese. I once thought it a good thing—less gossip in the workplace—but now, I just don't care what people think or feel. First off, it is my damn business. Second, Reese has been stellar at the job. He knows what I want, isn't afraid to go after it, and knows that maintaining a happy work life equals a superior homelife.

I nod. "Reese and I have been together more than a year. We had our challenges with my travels and crazy hours, but that has leveled out since I brought him into the fold."

"No unsavory arguments because you see too much of each other?"

I chuckle with a shake of my head. "I worried about

that too, but no. We're pretty good about switching business on and off when necessary."

"Good to see you happy," she says as Reese steps back inside.

"Radford has set everything in motion. Dale is making the appropriate calls in the office and to the banks. He'll call or text with updates as they come in."

I hold his confident stare for a beat then smile. "Thank you." Pushing back from the table, I rise and gather my belongings. "Cat, let's have dinner tonight. Bring Shayla." I stow my phone in my suit jacket. "Let me get some work done and then we can meet around seven."

She stands and gathers her laptop, pad, and pen. "That'd be nice. How about The Stinking Rose?"

"The garlic place?" I ask and she nods. I look to Reese and he shrugs. "See you there at seven."

In no hurry, we all trek toward the door. I take in Catarina's posture—still a touch fallen, but not as prominent as earlier.

Her actions were foolish but not done with malice. This much, I believe. Though she will have a major ding in her file and trust to make up with me, I know this slip is a huge learning moment for her. She won't make any such mistake again.

This morning, my stomach twisted in unease. Some instinctual part of me knew something was off. That issues would pop up in the aftermath of Beverly Prescott. Now that we have learned what that something is, the wringing has unraveled a bit. It is a disaster but a manageable one.

Beverly may have slipped through the cracks with her

flashy résumé, fabricated resources, and bright smile. But with her weaselly ways and assumption I wouldn't be so hands-on after hiring her, she got cozy too soon. Lucky for me, and thanks to my father, I had paranoia on my side.

I cut her out early. Shut her down before real damage could be done. Not that what she'd done hadn't tampered with Callahan Industries; her actions definitely made a sizable dent. But thanks to Reese, the problem was caught early. Authorities will handle Beverly Prescott and the banks will work hard to get the money back in the rightful accounts.

All things happen for a reason, they say. On occasion, I follow the falling dominoes to figure out what good comes from the bad. The trail confuses and amazes me. Had I not been with Reese, I would have never hired Beverly Prescott, and this whole mess wouldn't exist. But this catastrophe did take place. And Beverly Prescott wasn't the only person involved. This disaster would've still existed, regardless.

I *am* with Reese. Now, he isn't just my boyfriend and lover. He is my partner in every sense of the word. Him by my side—in life and business—makes me a better person, whole, in every way.

Reese is the good.

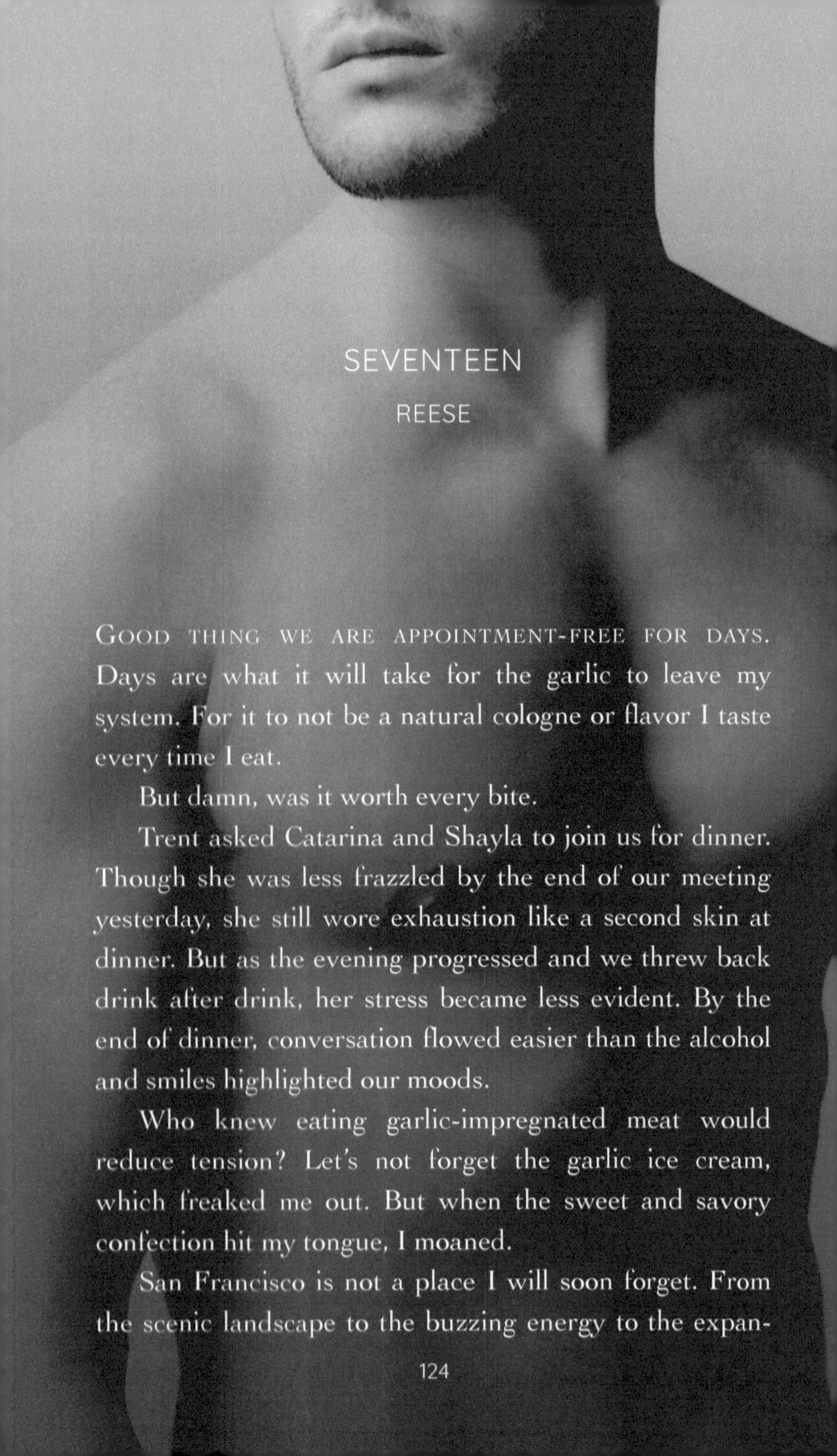

SEVENTEEN

REESE

Good thing we are appointment-free for days. Days are what it will take for the garlic to leave my system. For it to not be a natural cologne or flavor I taste every time I eat.

But damn, was it worth every bite.

Trent asked Catarina and Shayla to join us for dinner. Though she was less frazzled by the end of our meeting yesterday, she still wore exhaustion like a second skin at dinner. But as the evening progressed and we threw back drink after drink, her stress became less evident. By the end of dinner, conversation flowed easier than the alcohol and smiles highlighted our moods.

Who knew eating garlic-impregnated meat would reduce tension? Let's not forget the garlic ice cream, which freaked me out. But when the sweet and savory confection hit my tongue, I moaned.

San Francisco is not a place I will soon forget. From the scenic landscape to the buzzing energy to the expansive diversity. We will return, and I look forward to the day.

"Want to view the bridge from the lookout today?" Trent asks.

He tugs a black T-shirt over his head, the cotton snug against his muscular chest. The lean muscles of his biceps and forearms pop against the dark material. Stonewash denim hugs his hips, his sculpted ass, his thighs. His black hair product-free and finger-combed. A day's worth of scruff lines his sharp jawline. And when I meet his dazzling green eyes, I spy his cocked brow and the smirk lifting the corner of his mouth.

"Keep looking at me like that and we aren't leaving this suite."

I bite my lower lip and fight a smile. "Would that be so bad?"

In two quick strides, Trent stands between my denim-clad thighs. He grips my chin with his thumb and forefinger, tips my head back, and lowers himself until we are a breath apart.

"No, it wouldn't." He sucks my bottom lip between his. "But we should explore. Enjoy our time here." He releases my chin and steps back. "I want to see the city with you." He walks over to the closet and plucks his jacket from the hanger. "Visit the places I've missed out on because of meetings and schedules." Arms in the sleeves, he shrugs the jacket on and adjusts the collar. "And..." Rich-green irises meet my tawny browns, a hint of secrecy in his stare. "I may have something planned."

Rising from the bed, I pad to the dresser, grab socks,

then head to the closet for my sneakers. Shoes secure on my feet, I fetch my hoodie and tug it over my head as I walk past Trent out of the room.

"Fine," I say with dramatic flair. "But you need to feed me first." My stomach grumbles at the mention of food.

Hot on my heels, Trent wraps his arms around my waist and pulls my back flush to his front. He kisses a path up the side of my neck and I moan in response. On the next step, he sucks my earlobe between his lips and nibbles the soft flesh. My eyes roll closed as we stumble toward the door.

"Thought you wanted to go out," I say, voice low and throaty.

"I do." He releases my ear then peppers my neck in open-mouthed kisses. "But fuck if you aren't adorable when you're grouchy and demanding." Teeth mar the skin where my neck and shoulder meet, and then he steps back. "Couldn't help myself."

"Grouchy, huh?" I spin around to face him.

A smirk kicks up the corner of his mouth. "Don't forget demanding, too."

"Yeah, yeah," I tease. Fisting the lapels of his jacket, I haul him forward and kiss the hell out of him. When the kiss breaks, I rest my forehead on his and hold his gaze. "Feed. Me."

He laughs with a shake of his head. "As you wish."

Lacing his fingers with mine, he yanks me out the door and toward the elevator. As we enter the car, I curl into his side. Bask in his warmth. Inhale his crisp, fresh scent.

Revel in the love I share with this striking, fiercely loyal man.

With a ding, the doors slide open, and we enter the lobby. I slip on sunglasses as we exit the hotel and step onto the sidewalk. And on my next breath, I take in the man on my arm. Not his looks. Him.

Without Trent, I wouldn't be on the opposite side of the country, ready to explore. I wouldn't have this incredible life, one that gives me opportunity and purpose. I wouldn't know love. Real love. Love that eclipses everything.

Our relationship was rocky in the past. On unsteady ground every time Trent left me for work. I feared the long distance and time apart would end our love story. Turns out, neither of us was willing to let go.

Each day I wake up next to Trent, I thank the gods for him. Each time he says he loves me, I pray I never know a day without him.

EIGHTEEN

TRENT

SWEAT SLICKS MY SKIN AS I SQUIRM IN MY JACKET. With slow movements, I fan the leather lapel and pray Reese doesn't notice. Unfortunately, the crisp fall air doesn't hit my skin and is of no help for my anxiety-induced perspiration.

I have never been this nervous in my life. Not once.

Purchasing million-dollar properties—done with the flick of a wrist as I signed my name on the dotted line. Flying across the country and striking deals most would walk away from—done with confidence and the shake of a hand. Entertaining prospective clients and convincing them Callahan Industries is the place to be—done hundreds of times without breaking a sweat. The jitters I experienced interviewing Beverly Prescott are incompa-rable—although now I see them for what they were. A warning.

Still, none of them measure up. This… what I am about to do… I might throw up.

We step up to the rail and stare at the pristine view of the Golden Gate Bridge. The rusty-red bridge pops against the cloudless blue sky and I can't help but think how perfect the backdrop is for today. Every other time I visited San Francisco, clouds blanketed the bridge and fog horns howled in the distance. The most I'd seen of the bridge before today was the lanes while driving across or the peaks as I approached.

Call me superstitious, but getting this view today is a sign. A silent message from the universe telling me what I am about to do is the right move.

Please let it be the right move.

"We need pictures," Reese says, snapping me out of my introspection. He pulls his phone from his pocket and opens up the camera app. Handing it over, he says, "Take a few in case I blink."

I take several pictures of him before we trade places and he does the same. He sidles up to me, leans in close, and holds the phone up to take selfies of us. As Reese pockets his phone, I spot a couple not far from us taking pictures too.

"Be right back," I tell Reese. I approach the couple and offer to take a photo of them. As I hand back the phone, I ask, "Would you mind reciprocating?" I point over my shoulder toward Reese. "Except I'd like a video."

The woman narrows her eyes and stares for a beat before realization hits.

Yep.

"But can you make it look like you're taking pictures?"

Thrill has her bouncing in place. "Absolutely."

We walk back to where Reese waits and I hand her my phone before stepping up next to him by the rail. "I asked if they'd take pictures of us."

My favorite smile lights up his face as he wraps an arm around my shoulders. "Much better than a selfie."

Reese turns to face the woman with my phone, his smile brighter than the sun as wind whips his hair. I take a deep breath, dig in my pocket for the diamond-lined black band, and drop to one knee. The woman with my phone gasps and time stands still as Reese twists to face me.

I'd planned this day for weeks. Rehearsed my speech whenever Reese was out of earshot. Pictured this moment and his reaction countless times.

But every word I planned to say vanishes as I look up. Tears rim his addictive brown eyes. His Adam's apple bobs as he waits for what happens next. His knuckles bleach as he holds the rail tighter.

"Reese," I choke out, then swallow past the lump in my throat. "I memorized an epic speech for this moment. But as I kneel before you, I can't remember a damn word." I laugh without humor as I toy with the ring in my palm. "I've never known love like yours. Never thought it was possible to be loved by someone like you." Pinching the ring between my fingers, I hold it up. Offer him the most valuable token of my love. "What I do know is that I never want a day without you. I want you today, tomorrow, and every day that follows." Sucking in a sharp breath, I count to three and exhale. "Reese Triggs, will you do me the greatest honor and be my husband?"

In the periphery, the woman with my phone sniffles. I ignore her. Ignore everything except Reese, who is way too silent.

A new layer of perspiration layers my skin as I wait for Reese to answer, to react, to give some indication he heard my question. Hour-long seconds pass as he remains tight lipped. With each deafening second, I grow more concerned. Worry that his answer will be a resounding *no*. Nausea builds beneath my diaphragm. Bile creeps up my throat.

This moment may end us if his answer is no. This moment may be our final memory if he doesn't want to spend forever with me.

Before I chance a trip down heartbreak avenue, Reese drops to his knees in front of me. Frames my face with his hands. Stares deep into my eyes and swallows. And when the corners of his mouth tip up just the slightest bit, every dark thought and concern for our future floats away.

"Yes," he whispers. "A thousand times, yes."

He hauls me closer and crushes my lips with his. Kisses me without restraint. His hands fall away from my face, slip beneath my jacket, and band around my middle. Fisting the cotton of my shirt, he hugs me breathless. Says yes to my proposal again and again with his hands and lips on mine.

Reluctantly, I break the kiss. Remind myself we are in public and a random stranger is documenting this entire moment with my phone. But I'm not ready to leave the moment. Not yet. I drop my forehead to his. Lift a hand to his hair and toy with the curls. Give him a chaste kiss, followed by another.

"Love you," I whisper. "So damn much."

His lips curve into a soft smile. "Love you the most, future husband."

NINETEEN

REESE

I LIFT MY HANDS IN SURRENDER AND STARE WIDE EYED at the computer screen. "What the hell?"

The clicking of keys silences as Trent looks up and across the table. His brows pinch in obvious confusion as he regards my frantic state. "What's wrong?"

I drop my gaze back to the screen and watch in horror as pop-ups appear, one after another in rapid succession, flooding the screen. The cursor flies across the screen, but my hands are far from the touchpad. *Someone hacked my computer.* Someone is invading my files and doing who knows what. Stealing files. Downloading viruses or malware or Trojan horses. Whatever the hell is happening, it isn't good.

With the barest of touches, I spin the laptop and share my screen with Trent. "Something or someone is in my computer. Right now."

His eyes widen in shock. Then his phone is in his hand. He taps the screen three times before bringing it to his ear. An unfamiliar seriousness consumes his expression and stiffens his posture. The humorless CEO, that is who this is.

"Radford," he says, voice razor sharp. "I need you in my office. Now." Before Radford gets a word in, Trent disconnects the call. He points to the screen. "What were you doing just before that started?"

I take a deep breath and think past the panic. Close my eyes for one, two, three seconds, then focus my attention on Trent. "I opened the share drive and clicked Karina's folder. When I accessed the invoice spreadsheet, everything went crazy."

A knock sounds at the door before it swings open and Radford steps inside, closing it behind him. "Mr. Callahan." He nods to Trent, then repeats the gesture in my direction. "Mr. Triggs."

Trent's stern expression returns. "Radford, we have a problem." He twists the laptop in his direction as he approaches the table. "This occurred when Reese opened a file in the share drive."

"Shit," he mutters.

Pulling out a chair, he settles at the table with us. His fingers fly over the trackpad, tapping it every other second. Then his fingers are on the keyboard, striking the keys in rapid succession. He inches closer to the screen, narrows his eyes, and doesn't breathe. None of us do as he works.

And then he straightens in his chair. Sucks in a deep breath, his eyes finding ours on the exhale.

"I've locked down the computer and disconnected it

from the internet and server. Not sure how extensive the damage is, but this is bad," he says with a wince. He pushes away from the table and rises from the chair. "I need to grab a few things from my office. Not that it needs to be said, but don't touch the computer."

"Thank you, Radford," Trent says.

He exits the office, the quiet click of the door closing is deafening. The moment he is gone, Trent rests his elbows on the table and drops his head in his hands. His fingertips dig into his skin at a bruising level. With each inhale, I detect the jagged edge of his breathing. The worry over what this all means.

This invasion isn't minor. It was calculated. A plan laid out by a desperate and disgruntled woman. A woman wounded by her past and hell-bent on making others pay. A woman intelligent enough to cover her tracks after years of experience. The more we unearthed about Beverly Prescott, the less hope we had of her arrest.

Since our return from San Francisco last week, I learned Beverly's legal last name is Westcott and not Prescott. The last names were close. Close enough that calls verifying employment history were mishandled and the possible mishearing of the name was swept under the rug.

When I discovered that gem, I wondered how many other names Beverly used. Turns out, the more we dug — Callahan Industries, the attorney's office, and law enforcement — the more dirt we found.

Via facial recognition, we stumbled upon several arrests. All minor offenses that allowed her to go free in less than a year. A hundred dollars missing from the register, inventory counts off, numbers matching on paper but not adding up when the money counts were completed.

Her face matched each offense but not her name. Sally Graham. Danielle Roberts. Elenore Crowley. Those names were tied to jobs that paid under the table. Employers that didn't run her social security number or ask many questions. Employers that didn't take action until the losses started to pile up. Having Beverly arrested, the businesses were penalized for not following proper tax laws. I assume it was worth it for them in the end.

But that was only the beginning for Beverly.

When she'd gained enough felonious insight and stepped up her game, she started using her given first name. She recruited help. But there is one thing she didn't learn from her history of crime.

Don't fuck with Trent Callahan. Ever.

Reaching across the table, I tug a hand from his face. "May not seem like it, but everything will work out."

He lifts his gaze as his hand squeezes mine. A humorless laugh leaves his lips. "I'm losing confidence." His free hand scrubs down his face. "God, I want to believe. I want to trust that we'll find her and she'll go to prison long enough to never bother us again."

I lay my other hand on the table, palm up. He rests his hand in mine and I grip it tightly. Send him every ounce of strength and positivity. *We will get past this. And when we do, we'll be stronger than before.*

"Put your intentions out there. Say it with conviction.

Mean it." I lift his hand as I lean forward and press my lips to his skin. "We will get through this."

His eyes lock with mine as he digs deep for strength. I tighten my grip on his hands. Telling him with this simple touch I am his rock. His anchor. The person to hold and lift him up when times get rough. The person he can trust and lean on. Always.

And with each breath he takes, I witness the return of his power. His spine straightens. His shoulders square. The reluctance in his expression melts away. The muscles of his jaw flex. His gaze hardens.

After one last squeeze of his hands, I release him. "There you are." I wink. "My formidable fiancé."

He shoves back on his chair and stands in one quick, fluid movement. In the next breath, he is at my side, gripping my chin, tipping my head back. His mouth crashes down on mine. Mint mixed with desire sweeps over my tongue. As a moan spills from my mouth into his, he releases me and returns to his seat.

"Thank you," he says, swiping a thumb over his bottom lip.

My brows shoot up. "Uh... shouldn't I be thanking you?" I lick my lips and smile when I taste him there.

Light laughter floats through the air just as Radford returns. "Later." He winks in my direction, then gives his full attention to the head of tech security. "Let's hit this bitch where it hurts."

Radford eyes Trent, then me, purses his lips, and nods. "She won't make it out unscathed. Not this time."

Trent slaps him on the back. "Exactly what I needed to hear."

And then we spend several hours hunched over the computer, on the hunt for the grenade pin that started this entire war.

TWENTY

TRENT

Two days, three hours, and twenty-one minutes. That is how long it took to find the root of what Beverly Prescott—or whatever the hell her name is—set in motion.

Not only did we pinpoint the spyware she planted in our company server, we also picked up the location of her last log-on. With one phone call, she was in handcuffs and booked in the county jail hours later, awaiting further prosecution. My attorney warned she may not serve more than five years, but I had every confidence. Vincent started building a case against Beverly the minute I explained what she'd done. Although she committed significant and disastrous cybercrimes against Callahan Industries, the judicial system may look at the acts as less than worrisome.

She put on a stellar front during her interview. No doubt she will give the show of her life in front of a judge.

With her behind bars, we are in damage correction

mode. After more than a week, Radford and a few trusted others in security have cleaned up Beverly's destruction. Reports were filed with the bank and monies are being returned to the proper accounts. Each time we dig into Beverly's past, we encounter new evidence to present against her. And each time she is questioned by law enforcement, she turns more loose lipped.

Not wanting to take the fall on her own and hoping for a lesser sentence, her attorney advised she come forth with names of those in cahoots with her. When Beverly proclaimed Neal and Tracy were in on the scheme, I punched a wall.

Then I got to work.

Tracy and Neal were arrested on the same day as Beverly's confession. We'd been monitoring them since Reese unearthed their misappropriations. Since their activities hadn't picked up steam, I'd focused on Beverly first with the intent of dealing with them after.

But shit hit the fan fast.

When Beverly's confession hit my desk, fresh background checks were run on every employee under the Callahan Industries umbrella. No stone was left unturned; I wanted all the dirt, even the small deeds. If I lost several employees in the process, so be it.

But no one would fuck me over again.

Vincent says not to get my hopes up for more than five years and heavy fines. But after research of my own, when it is just me and Reese, I voice the penalties I want this woman and her minions to incur. Twenty-plus years in federal prison. Thousands of dollars in fines. A ding so profound on her record, no one will hire her. If she gets out. And with the support of former employers she swindled, my wishes may come true.

"It's too early to be thinking so loudly," Reese grumbles into the crook of my neck.

I rub a hand down his back and hug him closer. His hand slides up my abdomen, the diamonds in his engagement band glinting as they catch a sliver of morning sunlight. And damn, it is the sexiest sight.

Turning onto my side, I tangle my limbs with his and kiss his shoulder. "Sorry. Promise, I'm done." Short nails scratch up my back and I moan in his ear, my cock hardening against his hip. I take his ass in a bruising grip. "Mmm," I moan out. "Cock before breakfast. Perfect way to start the day."

And then I am on my back, arms pinned above my head as Reese takes my mouth with his. The kiss is punishing, hungry, addictive. He rocks his bare erection along my thick length—up and down, up and down— while sucking my tongue as if it were my cock.

Releasing my hands, he kisses his way down my body. Lips and tongue and teeth taste the lines of my collarbones, the stiff peaks of my nipples, the thin happy trail leading to where I want him most. As if he hears my thoughts, he licks the crown of my cock. Swirls his tongue around the swollen tip. Over and over. Teasing and tasting the drip of precum.

Fisting his hair, I lift his gaze to mine. "Be a good fucking boy and suck my cock." I raise my hips and jab his mouth with my dick. He flashes me a smirk, parts his lips, and takes me to the back of his throat. My back bows off the bed as he delivers a vicious rhythm. "Such a good…" *Slurp.* "Fucking…" *Scrape.* "Boy," I growl.

He pinches a nipple with one hand and fondles my balls with the other. His head bobs as he sucks me off with steady strokes. Releasing my nipple, he wraps a hand around the base of my shaft and kneads my cock for one, two, three strokes.

Then his soaked fingers are on my ass. Petting. Playing. Prodding the tight hole.

I groan. "No one likes a tease, Triggs."

Cold air slaps my wet cock as Reese releases me. I look at him in confusion and he snickers. Then he is on all fours and crawling up my body. He straddles my neck and shoves his erection between my lips. "Get me wet and I'll reward you."

I take his cock in my hand, part my lips, and lick the underside of him, root to tip. He clamps down on his bottom lip a second before I swallow him down. His tip hits the back of my throat and I gag. Relaxing my jaw and adjusting my position, I devour every inch of him with ease. Hand in my hair, he fucks my mouth without restraint.

As he swells further in my mouth, he pulls out, shimmies down my body and takes my mouth with his.

"Not yet," he whispers, more to himself than me.

He sits back on his haunches as I bring my knees toward my chest and out. Fingers dance over my cock in lazy, soft strokes. Then he cups my balls. Lifts and massages them. With his free hand, he spits in his palm then coats his dick.

The tip of his cock nudges my entrance, and I press into him. Encourage him to rock his hips forward. To take me, fill me, fuck me. When his crown breaches the rim, we moan simultaneously. Inch by glorious inch, he charges forward and stretches me to perfection. Saltiness filters through the air as our sweat-slicked bodies slap. His forearms bracket my head as his fingers fist my hair. Breath hot on my neck, his moans of pleasure consume my hearing and vibrate my chest.

"So close," he grunts in my ear.

I take his ass with both my hands and rock him harder. "Pump me full of cum, Triggs."

His hold on my hair tightens. "Got to stop… calling me… Triggs." He rocks his hips faster, his cock swelling as I process his words. "Callahan," he moans in my ear. Slowing his strokes, he lifts enough to meet my gaze. "Reese Callahan." And then he fills me with his cum.

I fist my cock and stroke. "Say it again," I demand.

"Reese Callahan."

"Fuck, that's the hottest thing to leave your lips."

Then his hand is around mine, both of us stroking my cock. Bringing me higher. Lifting me to the precipice. He whispers his future name one more time and I growl as hot cum spurts over my chest. My hand flies to his throat, my fingers digging into his flesh as I yank his mouth to mine in a bruising kiss.

Moans vibrate his chest, his throat, his lips as I swallow the taste of him. The kiss transitions from feral hunger to soft licks. A beat passes before he breaks the kiss, pushes up on his forearms, and stares at me like it's unimaginable that this is real. That this is our life.

"You're really going to take my last name?"

I never assumed Reese would change his name when we married. Taking someone's name is an outdated tradition. Although I prefer to dominate Reese in the bedroom, the thought of actually *owning* him is unnatural. He is his own person as much as I am my own person. Yes, he owns my heart, but it was my choice to hand it over.

When it comes to Reese, I never question his loyalty. I never question his love. But with this one thing, I will question him. Confirm he made this choice for himself and not because he thinks it is what I want. So long as I have him, I don't care what last name he bears.

He traces my jawline with his knuckles. "Yes. Is that okay?" Lines mar his forehead as his brows draw inward.

I smooth the worry lines in his expression with my finger. "Absolutely. As long as it's what you want."

Warm lips press to mine in a brief kiss. "It's what I want." He seals his vow with another kiss, this one slow and heated and heartfelt.

A whirl of thrill stirs in my belly. Heat blankets me from foot to crown as I hold his gaze. *Reese Callahan.* Goose bumps spread the length of my limbs as I shiver beneath him. *Damn, I love the sound of his name blended with mine.*

"Then it's yours for the taking."

EPILOGUE

REESE

February—one and a half years later

THE STICKY AIR BLANKETS MY SKIN AS I STEP INTO THE early afternoon sun. I shield my eyes and inhale the salty Atlantic air as I scan the beach. Not in search of Trent—he's locked himself away while he dresses for the ceremony. No, I am on the hunt for Peyton.

As if she hears my thoughts, she peeks over her shoulder and waves.

I trek across the sugar-fine sand barefoot and wrap her in my arms when I reach her. "Hey, sunshine." A squeal of laughter echoes in my ear as I spin her around. I set her back on her feet and extend a hand to Micah.

He takes it and pulls me into a shoulder-slapping hug. "Congrats, man."

"Thanks," I say as we break apart.

The three of us huddle together, one of Peyton's arms locked with mine and the other with her husband's. And it is exactly what I need. Familiar contact with someone close.

To say I am nervous would be an understatement. But marrying Trent isn't what has my stomach in knots. Life with him has been blissful. What has me on the cusp of puking is keeping him happy. Giving him what he needs. Staying his person through thick and thin.

Relationships are hard work. It doesn't take degrees or high IQs to figure that out.

The start of our relationship was rocky. Some days, I woke up wondering, *Is today the day he leaves and doesn't come back?* But he always came back. It was rough, but once we spilled our truths and shared our desires, our love life found its natural rhythm. After a couple blips, our nonromantic life leveled out as well.

Thank fuck.

"Doing okay?" Peyton asks as she hugs me closer to her side.

I scan the growing crowd. Many of them friends and family. And then there is the occasional familiar face from Callahan Industries. Dale and his husband. Radford and his girlfriend. Catarina and Shayla from the San Francisco office. Raul and Clint from the Chicago office. And there will be more to come.

Nodding, I bend and kiss her cheek. "Just ready to get this over with," I say with a laugh.

Peyton looks to Micah and a bright smile lights up her face. Then her eyes meet mine. "The minutes leading up to the ceremony feel endless. But before you know it, you'll be declared mister and mister Callahan. The stuff in the middle is kind of a blur." She leans into the huddle and drops her voice. "Thank god for pictures and videos."

"I'll second that," Micah states.

I open my mouth to voice it isn't the actual ceremony that has me jittery. But before I get a word out, the ordained minister interrupts us.

"Reese, time to get in position."

I throw her a smile. "Thank you, Frannie." Unhooking my arm from Peyton, I hug her and Micah again. "Go find your seats. See you both soon."

While they head for the chairs in the sand, I walk toward the house Trent and I rented for two weeks. On the first floor, I step inside the open Florida room and duck out of sight from the stairwell to the right. Any minute, Trent will walk down those stairs from our honeymoon suite and walk across the sand. And I will be twenty paces behind him.

For weeks after the proposal, we mulled over when and where to get married. Trent said we could travel to any location—in the States or internationally. Amazing as it would be to get married in another country and see the world, I didn't want the people closest to us to miss the day. Hosting two ceremonies was out of the question.

Work was the only reason we waited so long. That and the trial.

Days after Neal and Tracy were behind bars, Vincent asked the courts for a trial. He'd said, *"Trials don't always happen with cases such as this, but we want her locked up for good. And her lackeys."* With a few clicks of a mouse and swishes of a pen, we had a court date. Eight months out, but we had a hearing date. And in those eight months, we unearthed every wretched and despicable thing Beverly, Neal, and Tracy did.

In May last year, we endured a week in the courtroom. Days of testimony and boxes of evidence were heard and seen. And on the final day, the judge read the verdict and slapped the gavel on the sound block.

Guilty.

Not only was Beverly Westcott guilty of embezzlement in the first degree with Callahan Industries, she was also convicted for the other companies she pilfered. Altogether, she received seven embezzlement charges. Her penalty… fifteen years in federal prison for each count and ten-thousand dollars in fines for each count plus the monies stolen from each business.

Beverly would never see the outside world again.

As for Tracy and Neal, their penalties were less steep but still harsh. Ten years behind bars with no chance for parole and ten-thousand dollars in fines plus the monies they stole from Callahan Industries.

It'd been a relief to put the nightmare behind us and move forward with our lives.

Once we had a date set for the wedding, everything flowed together seamlessly. Trent found this gorgeous house in the Keys. He paid for travel, board, and food for all our guests—our closest friends and family sharing this house with us for a week. We decided on casual attire for the big day—white linen, bare feet, and nothing else. The only people we needed to coordinate dates with were the caterer and officiant. We opted for no flowers or fancy getups.

All that matters today is us.

Soft slaps carry on the breeze as Trent pads down the steps. I peek around the wall of my nook and see the back of him as he walks next to the swimming pool toward the private beach. When he reaches the far side of the pool, I step out and follow.

With each step forward, every worry I harbored over keeping this magnificent man happy evaporates with the tide. In our time together, we have overcome every obstacle thrown our way. And each time, we came out better than before. Stronger.

Challenges keep us on our toes, but love glues us together and never lets go.

Trent Callahan isn't some snobby mogul living at the top of an ivory tower. Trent Callahan is mine. My number one. The love of my life. My rock. And this is our beginning.

I walk through the sand down the makeshift aisle between white chairs. There is no wedding party, only us and Frannie at the front of the crowd.

"Hey," he whispers before a wide smile plumps his cheeks.

"Hi." I can't help but mirror his jubilance.

We take each other's hands and lock gazes as Frannie speaks. Every now and then, I listen in. Hear the words *love* and *devotion* and *forever.* And in this moment, nothing except us matters. Us and the here and now.

"Trent, whenever you'd like to start."

He gives my hands a light squeeze, then releases them and pulls a slip of paper from his pocket. Unfolding the paper, he swallows and studies the vows he wrote.

"There's a distinct line in my life. It divides the time before and after I met you." He takes a deep breath and meets my gaze. "Reese, you brought wonder and delight into my life. You revived me in a way I didn't know I needed. And after one night with you, I wanted more. I'd never wanted more until you." He inches closer, drops the paper, and takes my hands. "You give me purpose and drive and love. You make me want to be better." His forehead drops to mine. "You're it for me, and I am damn lucky to have found you."

Tears sting the backs of my eyes as I stare into his and fight the urge to kiss him. I suck in a sharp breath, hold it, and bask in the burn as my lungs beg for oxygen. On a shaky exhale, wetness coats the slope of my nose. The small tear falls, landing on our joined hands, and Trent tightens his hold.

"Love you," he says, a breath above a whisper.

Unable to resist, I drop a quick peck to his lips then straighten to my full height. Neither of us releases our hold on the other. Our eyes still firmly locked in place.

"Reese," Frannie says. "Whenever you're ready."

For weeks, I pondered over what to say in my vows. Weddings and public proclamations of love are unfamiliar territory. Though we don't hide our relationship from the world, we also don't put it on display. Boring as it is, we are just... normal.

Peyton and Micah's wedding is all I had to reference

when I pulled out pen and paper. I'd even gone so far as to look up *how to write wedding vows* online. Every time I picked up the pen and pressed the tip to paper, nothing happened. Minutes passed and the blue lines on the page blurred. The blankness of the page mocked me and made me question if I could really do this. Get married.

After throwing the pen across the room, I called Peyton. Begged for lunch or dinner to catch up. I didn't want to admit over the phone or through text that I was having trouble spilling my heart on paper. No, I'd needed face-to-face conversation. I'd needed to match her expression to the tone of her voice. I'd needed a boost of confidence and one of my best friends to tell me this anxiety over words was normal.

Over pizza, I'd confessed my fears. Over ice cream, she'd reassured me it would all flow naturally.

"Just speak from your heart. As long as you do that, nothing else matters."

After she'd said those words, I'd come up with a solution.

Instead of writing and rehearsing my vows, I chose to improvise in the moment. Let's just hope I don't ramble or make an ass of myself.

"Love was something I never thought I'd have." I hug his hands harder. "Someone to call my own. Someone to make me look at the world with new eyes. And then you appeared." Fresh tears prick my eyes as I sniffle. "You took my hand and whisked me away. I may have loved you on that first night." Trent trembles in my hold and I give him a soft smile. "From the beginning, it's been one adventure after another. Some tested us and our bond. Some made us prove we really wanted this, wanted each other, over everything else. And at the end of the day, our love always won." I release one of his hands and cup his cheek. "I never have and never will love anyone the way I love you, Trent Callahan. You give me strength and passion and constant inspiration. Because of you, I am a better man. Because of you, I stepped out of my comfort zone." A tear streaks his cheek and I swipe it with my thumb. "And because of you, I know love. Real love."

Before Frannie announces us husband and husband, my lips are on his. On a private beach in the Keys, I marry my best friend, my person. As cheers erupt around us, I smile against his lips. Melt into his touch. And sigh… because he is officially mine forever.

Reese was first seen in the Insomniac Duet as Peyton's roommate. If you haven't started the Bay Area Duet Series, the Click Duet kicks it off. Don't forget to check out Penny's novella (from the Inked Duet).

The Click Duet

High school sweethearts torn apart. When fate gives them a second chance, one doesn't trust they won't be hurt again. Through the Lens (Click Duet #1) and Time Exposure (Click Duet #2) is an angsty, second chance, friends to lovers romance with all the feels.

The Inked Duet

A man with a broken heart and a woman scared to put herself out there. Love is never easy. Sometimes love rips you apart. Fine Line (Inked Duet #1) and Love Buzz (Inked Duet #2) is a second chance at love, single parent romance with a pinch of angst and dash of suspense.

The Insomniac Duet

He was her high school bully. She was the outcast that secretly crushed on him. More than ten years later, he's her boss, completely oblivious to their shared past, and wants no one but her. More importantly, he doesn't understand her animosity toward him.

The Artist Duet

A tortured hero with the biggest heart and a charismatic heroine with the patience of a saint. Previous heartache has him fighting his desire to be more than friends with her. But she is everywhere, and he can't help but give in. The Artist Duet is an angsty, friends to lovers slow burn.

Penny

Everything familiar falls apart when her boss announces the sale of the tattoo shop, and that the new owner is on his way. When the bell over the door jingles and a familiar face appears, confusion and old feelings surface. He isn't just her brother's best friend and the guy she crushed on for most of her life... he is also her new boss.

Transcendental

A musician in search of his muse and a woman grieving the loss of her husband. Two weeks at an exclusive retreat and their connection rivals all others. Until she leaves early without notice. But he refuses to give up until he finds her again.

Distorted Devotion

Swept off her feet by love, life takes a dark, unexpected turn. Now the love of her life may be the cause of her death. Check out this gripping, romantic suspense.

Depths Awakened

A small town romance which captivates you from the start. Two broken souls have sworn off love. Vowed to never lose anyone else. But their undeniable attraction brings them together and refuses to let go.

Broken Metronome

When the music of the heart dies...

Broken Metronome is an angsty poetry collection full of heartache and the possibility of what may have been.

Slipping From Existence

Would it be so bad to slip from existence? Would it be so bad to give in to the darkness?

Slipping From Existence is a dark poetry collection centered around depression and coping while maintaining a brave face.

THANK YOU

Thank you so much for reading **Reese**, a novella in the **Bay Area Duet Series**. If you wouldn't mind taking a moment to leave a review on the retailer site where you made your purchase, Goodreads and/or BookBub, it would mean the world to me.

Reviews help other readers find and enjoy the book as well.

Much love,
 Persephone

Connect with Persephone

www.persephoneautumn.com

Subscribe to Persephone's newsletter

www.persephoneautumn.com/newsletter

Join Persephone's reader's group

Persephone's Playground

Follow Persephone online

instagram.com/persephoneautumn

facebook.com/persephoneautumnwrites

tiktok.com/@persephoneautumn

bookbub.com/authors/persephone-autumn

goodreads.com/persephoneautumn

amazon.com/author/persephoneautumn

pinterest.com/persephoneautumn

ACKNOWLEDGMENTS

To my family… Thank you for your endless support and cheering me on through this author journey!

Ellie and Rosa at My Brother's Editor! Your expertise is invaluable. Thank you for making my manuscript better than it was before I sent it to you. Just when I think I have things figured out, you prove me wrong 😂

Bloggers!! I would be nowhere without you! Thank you for reading my words and promoting my books all over the internet. YOU ROCK!!

To my ARC review team! Thank you for taking a chance on me. Thank you for wanting to read my books and supporting me. And thank you for every review—they are GOLD! Without any of you, things would be so much different.

To every author I have bugged with questions. It amazes me how wonderful the writing community is. To belong to a community where every person wants everyone to thrive and succeed… I love it and you!

Readers are the best humans! Thank you to each and every one of you for reading my words. For choosing one of my books, thank you times a million. If I could hug you all, my tentacle arms would squeeze you tight.

And if this is your first Persephone Autumn story… thank you for taking a chance on my words. I hope you loved Reese and Trent.

ABOUT THE AUTHOR

USA Today Bestselling Author Persephone Autumn lives in Florida with her wife, crazy dog, and two lover-boy cats. A proud mom with a cuckoo grandpup. An ethnic food enthusiast who has fun discovering ways to vegan-ize her favorite non-vegan foods. If given the opportunity, she would intentionally get lost in nature.

For years, Persephone did some form of writing; mostly journaling or poetry. After pairing her poetry with images and posting them online, she began the journey of writing her first novel.

She mainly writes romance and poetry, but on occasion dips her toes in other works. Look for her non-romance publications under P. Autumn.